CHOSEN BY DADDY

PEPPER NORTH

AUTHOR'S NOTE:

The following story is completely fictional. The characters are all over the age of 18 and as adults choose to live their lives in an age play environment.

This is a series of books that can be read in any order. You may, however, choose to read them sequentially to enjoy the characters best. Subsequent books will feature characters that appear in previous novels as well as new faces.

CHAPTER 1

Parking her car outside the sleek, downtown business, Carina Richmond pulled her large purse onto her lap. Dipping her hand to retrieve her wallet, Carina pulled out a black card that was tattered and worn around the edges. The red letters had faded slightly over the years, but she still could read them clearly, I choose you. Flipping it over, she ran her fingers over the imprinted name, Luca Ricci.

Before she could chicken out, Carina pushed open her door and headed for the entrance. All she could do was ask, perhaps he would help. Cold air rushed out to greet her as the door opened automatically. Shivering, Carina froze for a moment before forcing herself to cross the threshold.

A large desk sat in the middle of the foyer. Hearing her heels click on the marble floor, Carina approached the elegant woman. "Good afternoon. I'm afraid I don't have an appointment, but I would like to see Luca Ricci."

Immediately, the receptionist smiled her regrets. "I'm afraid Mr. Luca is not seeing anyone today. Would you like to set up an appointment?"

"I have this," Carina shared, holding up the card so that the woman could read it before flipping it over to show the name. "If you would tell Luca that Carina Richmond is here, I would appreciate it. I'm here on an urgent matter."

"I'll contact his secretary. Would you like to take a seat in our reception area?" The woman suggested without blinking an eye at the tattered card in Carina's hand.

She nodded and walked slowly over to the grouped chairs and couches. Sitting, she discovered that they were designed for their look and not for comfort. Carina perched awkwardly on the edge of one chair. She did not touch the magazines perfectly arranged on the coffee table. The business and real estate titles did not interest her.

"Ms. Richmond?" A smooth female voice greeted her. When Carina nodded, she continued, "Mr. Ricci has made room in his schedule for you. If you would follow me?"

Carina studied the woman as she trailed her to the elevators and on the ride to the penthouse level. She was beautiful. Her long hair pulled back in an elegant chignon to match the expertly tailored black skirt and jacket. When her escort did not speak, Carina stood quietly and exited after her on the thirteenth floor.

Walking down the wide hallway, Carina marveled at the beautiful décor. She'd always known Luca Ricci would be a success. In his powerful family, nothing else would be accepted and Luca had been determined even as a young man.

A dark-haired man lounged against the doorway at the end of the hall. Even to Carina's inexperienced eyes, his suit was more expensive than an entire month of her teacher salary. Chiseled muscle encased in a suave wrapper, he was pure danger.

"Carina," Luca greeted her. His voice deep and smooth flowed over her like melted chocolate. Stepping out of the doorway, he gestured for her to enter before closing the door behind them. "You kept it."

"You told me to," she answered quickly before holding it out to him. She'd always known that the card would be good for one favor, no more. A Valentine card from him when they were in eighth grade. He'd been fifteen to her thirteen. Carina had skipped forward two years of the private school they'd attended.

"You never asked me any questions. I'd guessed that you'd thrown it away."

"I knew better than that. Your family…" Her voice trailed off. The Ricci family controlled their city. To her surprise, he didn't follow up on her statement but simply accepted the card.

Sitting on the edge of his enormous, walnut desk, Luca motioned her towards one of the elegant chairs in front of him before asking asked, "What favor brought you here? It must be important after all these years."

"I'm a teacher now." Carina didn't move. She stood poised by the door.

"Yes. You finished a couple of degrees at the university and worked at an engineering firm before deciding to use your teaching credentials. You've taught first and second grade for three years at Hardin Elementary," Luca provided

Carina nodded before processing his words. How did he know these things? And why? Shaking off those questions, she proceeded as if he hadn't spoken. "I have a student. She is delightfully brilliant and more eager to learn than anyone I've ever had in class before."

"It sounds like she could be you several years ago," Luca commented.

"Maybe. But she is in trouble. Or her family is. Susana needs an operation. Her mother works in your IT department. When health insurance refused to pay, the mother, in desperation, embezzled a large sum."

"Maria Perez," Luca provided without searching for the name. His eyes hardened as his posture straightened.

"Charges have been pressed and I believe she is currently awaiting a preliminary hearing."

"Susana needs her mother, and she needs this operation. Without it, she will slowly lose her vision." Carina paused, unsure how she should proceed. He was not sympathetic to the woman who had stolen money from his company—from the Ricci family.

The silence became deafening. When Carina could stand it no longer, she quietly stated, "I would like to use the favor that you gifted me so many years ago."

"You wish me to drop the charges against Maria Perez?" He asked before standing to approach Carina's position.

"Yes. And I would like you to fund her surgery and the recovery that follows." Carina forced her hands to stop fiddling with the clasp of her large purse. She wanted to present a calm and reasoned image to keep this professional and not personal. Holding her breath, she waited for his answer.

Luca walked around his desk to type short message into his computer before meeting her eyes. "You ask a lot for this favor, Valentine. In return, I will ask for everything."

A quiet knock on the door drew their attention. "Come in, Helen," Luca directed his tone brisk and professional. Carina stepped away from the door as it opened, and a capable-looking woman entered with the file. She smiled at Carina as she passed before handing the paperwork to Luca and departing. Within a minute, they were alone once again.

"Come sign, Carina," Luca directed. He opened the folder and selected a pen from his desk. Holding it out to her, he waited.

"What is this?" She asked walking forward to stare at the single sheet of paper. In big at the top, she read, "Marriage

License." Her gaze flew to meet his deep brown eyes. "You want me to marry you?"

"You will be mine, legally and forever. There will never be a divorce, separation, or divided home. You will live under my control and my guidance. Your nursery has already been created."

"Nursery? You want me to have your child," she asked, totally floored. Luca had never wanted for dates. The girls had been all over him in school. Glancing over his handsome face, she doubted that he had any lack of volunteers to fill his bed.

"No, Carina. The nursery is for you," he said, tapping on his computer. Seconds ticked by scaring the wits out of her before he turned around his screen to display the e-books that she had downloaded to her tablet. All ordered under a fake profile in a paranoid attempt to ensure the school district didn't fire her for her choice of reading material.

"How did you…" Her voice trailed away as her eyes scanned the list of age play books that she had devoured over the last few years. Her eyes lifted to meet his as she struggled to find a way to cover this up.

"I've always known that I needed to be a Daddy for Little girl. Just as I've always known that you were that Little girl."

"You've been spying on me?" Her voice rose with a panicked tone.

"You're mine. You've always been mine. All I needed you to do was to ask your favor. Sign the paper, Carina. It's time you came home." His large hand extended the pen to her as he pointed to the line on the marriage certificate where she should sign.

Carina forced herself to take several deep breaths to calm down. Focusing on the reason that had brought her here, she reminded herself that she'd expected his price would exceed the small card that she'd returned. She stiffened her back and forced herself to ask, "I want it in writing that you will drop all charges against Maria Perez, that you will never reenact these, and that you will fund the surgery and recovery of Susana Perez."

"I will promise you those things, but I will demand your trust."

Staring at his unyielding expression, Carina knew that she would have to accept his word. She took small steps forward, trying to convince herself that everything would be okay. As she took the pen from his fingers, she met his eyes once again. "May I trust that you will care for me as well?"

"Caring for you has just become my number one priority."

His answer sent a shiver down her spine as she set the pen on the license and signed her name. As soon as she dotted the i on her last name, Luca pulled her into his arms and lowered his lips to hers. Carina clung to his shoulders as his dominate kiss ignited her arousal. The attraction that she'd fled from for so many years burst into flames as Luca kissed her like no one ever had before.

CHAPTER 2

Luca wrapped an arm around his fiancée's waist. He could feel Carina's muscles trembling against him as she presented a calm front to the massive crowd gathered at their engagement party. His family did nothing by halves. Every mover and shaker in the city had been delighted to receive their invitation from the Ricci family. It was important to maintain a good relationship with those in power.

"Breathe, Carina," he directed as he smiled and nodded to accept the congratulations being thrown their way as they walked through the parted crowd to join his parents on the stairs. Helping her step up to the landing, Luca steadied the woman he'd planned to marry years ago.

Accepting two champagne flutes from the offered tray, he smiled as his father began to speak. His mother, standing by the elder Ricci's side, was visibly pleased with her son's selection of a wife. Their lifestyle was not known outside their family. Just like all the other secrets kept by the powerful family, no one needed to know. Carlota's nursery had just been redecorated in celebration of another Little girl joining the family. His mother loved the beautiful room where she spent most of her time.

Carina, of course, wasn't privy to this information. Luca smiled inwardly. He would enjoy watching her learn about his family and her place in it. When his father finished speaking, the crowd applauded enthusiastically as they called their congratulations to the young couple.

Caressing the sensitive skin of her inner arm as his fingers glided down to weave together with hers, Luca took a step forward. He smiled at her in approval as she matched his movement. Raising his champagne glass, Luca addressed the crowd, "Thank you for coming to celebrate with Carina and I. I have waited to marry this beautiful woman since she sat in front of me in math class. Our marriage will be worth the wait." He raised his glass as cheers of goodwill filled the air. As he sipped the exquisite bubbly drink, everyone joined him.

A few moments later, the band began to play. Leading Carina to the clearing floor, he swept her into their first dance. Her body followed his lead perfectly. "I know this is a long night, sweetheart. In about an hour, we'll be able to leave."

"Maria Perez called me today. The surgery is scheduled for next week. I would like to be there." The words tumbled from Carina's mouth, attesting to her nervousness.

"My offer for private nursing staff has been accepted. They will keep us updated as to Susana's progress. You will have no contact with the family from now on," he replied softly, maintaining his social smile to those beginning to join them on the dance floor.

Her white teeth closed on her bottom lip. Luca realized that she was literally biting back the words she wished to say. She was learning. His hand glided down her back to rest at the curve of her sweet bottom. He had not had to spank her yet. It was coming. Her rebellion was brewing. He'd always loved her inner fire. She didn't reveal it often.

* * *

Carina's slow burn of indignation had built into an inferno by the time Luca followed her into her apartment. She was tired of everything: smiling when she didn't want to smile, wearing the elegant dress and heels that had arrived on her doorstep with the instructions to wear them tonight, feeling like a total fraud while everyone congratulated them on their love match. Now, he had invited himself into her apartment when all she wanted to do was collapse on her bed.

Dropping her purse on the entry table, Carina turned to Luca and coolly informed him, "I would like you to go now, please. I'm tired and want to go to bed. I need to be up early to create lesson plans for my class."

"Your class has been assigned to another teacher. You will not be returning," Luca informed her.

"What? You can't do that! I love those kids. I love my job. I'm not going to stop teaching!"

"I'm sure the principal has selected a fine teacher to take your place. There will be an adjustment period for the students but they're young," Luca answered smoothly.

Unable to even speak to him, Carina grabbed her purse and opened it up to pull out her phone. Searching through her contacts, she looked for the principal's number. She was so angry. It took her a couple of tries through the alphabet to find his name. Pressing the button, she turned away from Luca and waited for him to answer.

"Carina? It's three o'clock in the morning? What's going on?" The puzzled voice of her principal made her realize how late or early it was.

"My apologies, Mr. Sanders. I was just told that a new teacher would be taking my class. I was so upset I didn't stop to look at the clock."

"I was surprised to hear from the superintendent that you

would not be returning to class in the middle of the year. My first concern was that you were ill. I was very relieved to hear that you were getting married. The Ricci family supports in many ways. I understood instantly that your role in the family would not allow you to teach full-time."

"Actually Mr. Sanders, that's not correct. I was not consulted as these decisions were made. I Would like to keep my job," Carina rushed to assure him.

"I'm sorry, Carina. You were an excellent teacher and your students loved you. I cannot go against the dictates of the superintendent. You're welcome to contact him but I'm afraid you will find that his first priority is to maintain the district's community support. Now if you'll excuse me, I'll try to get a couple more hours of sleep."

The silence that followed underlined the finality of the decision. She lost her job because of him. Whirling to face Luca, she discovered that he had taken a seat on the couch and was waiting patiently. Infuriated that he had made himself at home while her life was falling apart, Carina exploded, "Who the hell do you think you are? They gave my job away. I loved that job. I studied hard to be the best teacher ever and you destroyed that."

Fumbling with the large solitaire on her finger, Carina desperately worked to pull it off. Stiffly, she held it out to Luca, "Take this. Our wedding is off. I will not marry you."

Ignoring the ring, Luca pulled out his phone and selected a contact. He pressed a button to put the phone on speaker so that she could hear easily. "Sainte Genevieve's hospital. How may I direct your call?"

"Good morning, I need to speak to the director of surgery. I know it's early, but he will speak to me. Please tell him that Luca Ricci is calling."

Carina took three steps forward as the operator responded, "Thank you for calling, Mr. Ricci. I will get the director on the phone. One moment, please."

When she heard the music began to signal that he had been placed on hold, Carina asked, "What are you doing?"

"I'm canceling Susana's operation. I warned you that your favor came with stipulations. My wife is unable to have a full-time job. I took care of this for you as I will take care of everything in the future. However, if you are reneging on your decision, there is no need for me to pay for Susana's operation. My next phone call will be to the police captain. The paperwork against Maria Perez has been sealed in his office and can be enacted at any time in any year."

"You can't do this!" Carina protested. The innocuous music playing loudly from his phone frazzled her nerves. Rocked by the implications of his phone call, Carina dropped into a chair and stared at him in horror.

"I can. And I will. You will be mine in all senses of the word," Luca informed her calmly.

His tone completely devoid of all emotion scared her. "Luca, you're frightening me. I know you can't be this unfeeling. Can't you help Susana just because it's the right thing to do?"

"Susana's operation and aftercare will last for years. The financial burden of shouldering the costs will be a drain on my business. I'm willing to pay for all of this, for you," he answered, holding her gaze with his hard eyes.

"So, I have to give up my life completely to help her?" When he nodded, she exhaled a long shuddering breath. Carina met his eyes straight on. "Are you going to hurt me?"

"I will care for you completely, Little girl. That will mean rewards when you are good and consequences when you are bad."

Luca's tone was even and sounded ridiculously reasonable to her ears. Pushing, Carina asked, "Consequences? What? Like spankings?" she laughed in mockery.

"Yes, and more."

His stern tone erased any amusement from her face. "You're not joking, are you?"

"No," Luca confirmed. "You will be my Little girl for the rest of your life."

"Forever?" she echoed. "There could be a divorce."

"There will be no divorce. The ramification of using your favor is life as my wife and Little girl."

A click sounded on the phone as the doctor picked up the line, "Mr. Ricci?" the deep voice asked.

Carina stared in horror as her handsome fiancé turned off the speaker and raised the cellphone to his ear. She listened as Luca greeted the director. Closing her eyes, Carina swallowed hard. She couldn't allow Susana to lose her chance for a full life. "I'll do it. Take care of Susana."

"Director, I apologize for waking you early this morning. I'm afraid we've had a miscommunication here. All funding is still in place for Susana Perez. Please have the best surgeon care for her," Luca requested smoothly.

The rest of their conversations floated over Carina's head. None of it mattered. Luca was in control. She'd known the moment she'd used that card that there would be no turning back.

A shiver ran down her spine. Little girl. She'd had so many fantasies of being cared for as the Daddies did in those books on her reader. She peeked at Luca between her lashes. She'd seen him react cruelly to those that hurt others or didn't follow his guidelines. Could she submit to him so fully?

"We will not have this conversation again. Your decision has been made," Luca sternly warned. "You have earned your first punishment." He rose from the couch with athletic ease.

Squatting in front of her, Luca smoothed a hand down her slim calf to the strap of her silver pumps. With a few deft motions, he unfastened and removed the high heeled shoe which had become so uncomfortable to wear. His hands rubbed over her aching arch.

"Little girls don't dress up in such troublesome adult fanciness often. I promise you will be more comfortable in your nursery," he reassured her warmly when she moaned in delight from his foot rub.

Fascinated by this side of him, Carina watched as he removed her other shoe and treated her to the same caring treatment. Setting the shoes safely under her chair, Luca rose smoothly to his feet before extending a hand to help her stand as well.

"Stand up, Valentine."

"Why do you call me, Valentine?" she asked, grasping at any way to delay the punishment she knew was coming.

"With that card, I asked you to be mine. Giving it to you on February fourthteen, makes you my Valentine," he explained before extending his hand again and repeating, ""Stand up

To her dismay, Carina noticed her hand trembled as she placed it in his. She wanted to appear strong and in control but inside, she was so scared. Luca bolstered her up to her feet with a gentle tug and pulled her body against his to hold her tightly against his warm body. Holding herself stiffly against him, Carina tried to hold on to her anger at him, but the kindness undid her. Tears burst from her eyes as his hand stroked up and down her spine.

"You're okay, Carina mine. I'll take good care of you. I promise," Luca soothed. He leaned slightly away from her to press a soft kiss to her lips. It was not the passionate kisses the couple had exchanged previously. When he lifted his mouth from hers, Luca pressed a kiss to the tip of her nose. "Now, let's get this scratchy gown off you so we can put your punishment behind you."

Baffled by her own reaction, Carina nodded obediently. She rotated as he turned her shoulders. Stilling, she felt him unfasten the long zipper that spanned down her torso. Her hands pressed the bodice to her breasts as it loosened.

"Hands by your sides, Little girl. There is no hiding from Daddy," Luca sternly corrected.

When she slowly lowered her arms, Carina felt her dress cascade to the floor, leaving her dressed only in a wisp of lace serving as her thong. Her face heating, she knew she was blushing furiously. The dominant man hooked his fingers under the side pieces of her underwear and slid the beautiful decoration to her ankles.

"Step out of your pretty adult things, Carina," Luca directed, holding one of her arms to stabilize her. He led her to the large upholstered ottoman in the center of the room. "On your hands and knees, Little girl."

Carina glanced over her shoulder at him. Surely, he didn't mean for her to crawl onto the padded surface. When he nodded and urged her forward, she moved automatically into position as his hands guided her.

"Lay your cheek on the leather," he directed as he pressed between her shoulder blades.

"What are you going to do to me?" she hesitated to ask.

"Punish you."

"Spank me?" she squeaked.

"Yes, Carina. Into position, now." His hand impelled her shoulders to the cold padding and held her pinned in place. "You threatened to leave me, Carina. That is a serious offense. Normally, I would punish you very severely." His free hand softly traced over her bottom, exploring her body. To her horror, his finger pressed between her buttocks to lightly circle around her anus. "If this were to happen again, I would know that you have naughtiness inside you that needs to be washed out. Have you ever had an enema, Carina?"

"No. You wouldn't do that to me!" she struggled to sit up and shift away from his touch.

"You will have enemas, Carina. As your Daddy, I know

that your tummy needs special treatment so that you can be healthy. Those cleanings will be much different than a punitive one. Tonight, I will simply spank you."

Carina bucked against his hold as Luca's fingers moved lower. She didn't want him to discover her secret, but he already knew. Her body had responded to his dominance with a flood of arousal. Slick juices coated her pink folds and upper thighs.

"You are very wet, Little one. Perhaps afterward, I will help you find the pleasure you seek," he suggested.

Before she could process his words, Luca moved those tantalizing fingers away. Smack, smack, smack! His hand landed heavily on her pale bottom. Burning pain lanced through her, taking Carina's breath away. She struggled to move again but was anchored in place by his restraining hand as the other continued to deliver stinging swats to her bottom.

"Luca! Luca, no! Stop!" Heat built under his punishing touch. Carina suspected that her bottom was deep red. She panted between pleas for him to stop. Her words fell on deaf ears. He did not respond. Tears began to pour from her eyes to puddle on the smooth leather under her cheek. "I'm sorry, Luca! I'm sorry!" she called desperate for the spanking to end.

Finally, he answered, his deep voice shocking her with his calmness, "Call me, Daddy when we are alone, Carina."

"D...Daddy?" she repeated. Her voice stuttering with her sobs.

Luca's hand paused and tenderly rubbed her hot bottom. "Yes, Little girl. Just like that. You deserve a reward for being brave. Count for me for the last five swats."

"I don't want five more swats," she sobbed against the leather.

"Daddy will always know what you need. Count for me," he reminded her. His heavy hand rose and dropped on her small bottom. Luca paused waiting and smiled when Carina announced "One" followed by a sob.

"That's my good girl. You're learning so fast," Luca complimented and spanked that tender line between her buttock and her upper thigh.

Carina bit down on two knuckles trying to stifle the scream she felt welling in her throat. Luca's hand landed again in the same spot making her lurch forward to try to get away. "Please," she whimpered as his strength held her easily in place.

"Don't forget to count, Valentine. You don't want your spanking to last forever," he answered softly and lifted his hand to punish the same spot three times in a row.

"Three!" she screamed as his landed again.

"Two," he corrected before swatting another area.

"Two," she rushed to agree. Struggling to talk, Carina announced the last three spanks he delivered to her bottom. When he released the pressure on her shoulders, she crumpled shaking to the ottoman. Trying to draw together her whirling thoughts, Carina begged, "Please, Luca. Don't do this to me."

"Turn over, Little girl." His voice was low and even. The heavy hand which had held her so firmly in place now helped lift and rotate her body.

Carina hissed as her punished flesh touched the cold leather. She could feel the wetness of her tears under her shoulders. Trying to hide from his knowing eyes, Carina threw one arm over her face. She snatched it away as he pitched her throbbing bottom in warning.

"Never hide from your Daddy, Little girl."

She nodded without even knowing what she agreed with. Carina watched the dangerous man arrange her body as he wanted. Unsure what he planned, she was relieved that her punishment seemed to be over. Luca moved to kneel next to the ottoman, taking a position between her thighs. Automatically, she tried to pull her legs together to hide her more most intimate space. His hands curved cruelly around her inner thighs to hold her in place.

"Little girls need pleasure as well as punishment. I will wait to claim you completely until we are married. Call me an old-fashioned man." Luca laughed at his own joke. "I won't however wait to sample your body," he informed her as he lifted one slender thigh over his shoulder and leaned down to slide his tongue through her juices.

His caress seemed shocking. There were no caresses or kisses preceding his mouth capturing her intimately. Somehow, it felt more controlling. Her breasts ached for his touch. Carina moved her hands to caress them herself and froze as Luca lifted his lips and stared down her body. Immediately, she linked her fingers and looped them behind her head, moaning as his wicked mouth and tongue devoured her.

She wanted to look away, but his eyes held hers. The muscles of her inner thighs twitched in reaction as she struggled to hold herself in place. Carina always had difficulty orgasming. Her whirling mind always got in the way of her giving in to the sensations. She knew just his mouth on her would never get her there.

"Little girl, you are resisting your Daddy," he murmured against her body.

"I'm sorry," tumbled from her lips.

"Daddy knows what his Little girl needs. Everything is in my control," Luca answered confidently. His lips sealed around her clit and he sucked that small bundle of nerves confidently into his mouth. Instantly, pleasure slammed through her body and she arched against his mouth.

Luca gentled his intimate care, prolonging her gasps of pleasure. Lifting his head, he waited until her vision centered on him once again before licking his lips deliberately. Carina could feel her body spasm in reaction to his utter masculine enjoyment of her body. She had known Luca would be a passionate lover, but he surprised her by being focused on her enjoyment.

"Time for bed, Valentine." He rose athletically to his feet and lifted her in his arms. She could feel his rigid shaft against her body. Forcing herself to resist the allure of his hardness against her, Carina held herself stiffly against Luca. Carrying her to the restroom, he stood her before the toilet. "Go potty, Carina."

Panicked, she looked at him in disbelief. "I can't go in front of you."

"What is more intimate, Carina—my mouth between your thighs or my presence in the room while you empty your bladder?"

"What?" she tried to process his words, but her mind was too frazzled from the shock of her spanking and subsequent climax.

"There is nothing private for you, Little one. Go potty," he commanded. Turning slightly away from her, Luca opened a cabinet and pulled out a washcloth.

Carina stood frozen in place. Could she do this? Her student popped into her mind. She had started this to help Susanna. Now staring at Luca, the child was far from her mind. Luca loomed through her awareness. Shocked by her thoughts, she automatically sat on the toilet. The first sound from the bowl startled her and she looked up at Luca who stood at the sink.

When she finished and popped up, Luca beckoned her to join him, "Come, Carina."

Drawn by her reflection, Carina stared at her makeup and tear-stained face. The emotional toil of the evening was etched in her skin. Quickly, she covered her face and turned away from him. How had she not known how awful she looked?

His powerful hands closed over her shoulders and he prevented her instinctive movement. "Close your eyes," he commanded. Without pausing to allow her time to follow his instructions, Luca wiped the warm cloth over her face.

Instinctively, she followed his directions. The feel of the soft terry brushing her face zapped the last of her ability to withhold any part of herself from him. Carina leaned against his body accepting his support.

"Ah, Carina, mine. Caring for you is everything I've dreamed of for years. Let's pop you in the shower and then it's way past your bedtime, Little girl."

Without argument, Carina allowed him to help her step into the shower stall once the water had warmed. She quickly washed herself as he watched through the steamy glass doors. Surprising herself, Carina swiped a hand over the barrier between them when her view was obscured. Was she hoping that he was still there or gone?

"Rinse off, Little girl. It is time for bed," Luca instructed, pushing away from the vanity to grab a large towel from the rack.

She watched him approach slowly. Luca focused completely on her. Carina wasn't used to being the center of anyone's attention. Even when dating other men, phones or others around distracted those around her. The glass door slid open and she quickly shut off the water.

"Do you even have a phone?" she blurted as his hands wrapped the towel around her body.

"I do." Luca rubbed her skin softly with the thirsty cotton. Her swift inhale when he reached her punished bottom put a small smile on his face.

"I'm not going to let you beat me," she told him fiercely.

"You are mine to do with as I please," he warned as that fond expression hardened. "You are mine, Little girl. You will be much happier once you accept that."

Carina swallowed hard under his dominant stare. It was so hard to be rebellious with him close to her. Without meaning to, she nodded, accepting his advice.

"Come. It is time for bed," Luca announced, tossing the damp towel over the shower glass. He wrapped an arm around her nude body and directed Carina to the bedroom.

"Pick out something soft to wear," he suggested, rubbing her still stinging bottom softly. He watched as she knelt by the bottom drawer of her dresser and burrowed to the bottom. Rejecting lacy, frilly garments, he nodded his approval of the soft cotton nightshirt.

Taking it from her, Luca shook out the fabric and looped it over her head. He tenderly guided her hands into the short sleeves and smoothed it over her body. His touch was tender as if he truly cared about her. Lifting the corner of her comforter, Luca instructed, "Slide in, Little girl. Best to sleep on your tummy tonight."

"Luca…"

"Daddy, Little girl," Luca corrected as he helped her into bed.

"Is this real?" she whispered, needing to double check.

Leaning over, he pressed a kiss on her forehead. "Daddy will take care of you from now on, Little girl." He reached across her body to snag a well-loved yellow stuffed kitty. "Hold on to your friend, Carina. Sleep well."

As he stood, Carina realized that he still wore his tuxedo from the evening. His tie and coat still in place, Luca's formal dress made her feel even more Little. Her last glimpse of him was silhouetted in the doorway when he turned off her lights.

CHAPTER 3

"**D**affy, how did he know I still slept with you?" Carina whispered to the stuffie who had been her companion for years. Not her childhood toy but a spur of the moment purchase, Daffodil had waited for her at the checkout of the pharmacy near her university. Sick with a bad cold and feeling very alone away from home, Carina had placed the cheerful kitten in her basket.

"He seems to know everything."

Just saying that aloud made it feel so real. Luca did know everything about her. He knew at a glance that she slept with the stuffie even when it was tucked high on the headboard as if it were a decoration. Her hand smoothed over the soft nightshirt. How had he known that she had this at the bottom of the drawer? He hadn't responded to the pretty lacy teddies in her dresser.

"He wants me to call him Daddy."

The sweet stuffie just smiled at her like always. Carina inhaled sharply as her phone rang on her bedside table. She hadn't set it there. Nabbing the small device, she answered, "Hello?"

"Good morning, Little girl. Did you sleep well?" Luca's deep voice curled around her.

Carina's body reacted instantaneously. She curled onto her side to pull Daffy to her breasts. "Hi," she answered softly.

"I am coming to pick you up, Carina. We have an appointment and then, I will take you to see your nursery and perhaps spend a bit of time with my parents."

"What kind of appointment?" she squeaked. "I don't think that I can sit down to ride in the car, Luca."

"A perfect reminder to behave," he observed before adding, "Punished bottoms are more common than you'd think at my home."

Searching for anything to distract her whirling thoughts, Carina blurted, "You live with your parents?"

"You will see everything in an hour. I am here now to help you get ready," he announced as she heard the sound of keys unlocking her door.

With an eep, Carina jacknifed to sit in bed. She heard his solid footsteps in the hallway, and she debated whether to get up or stay in bed to hide. He walked through the doorway while she still attempted to make up her mind.

"How'd you get a key?" she asked, buying herself time.

"Good morning, Little girl. It's time to get up. We have some busy days ahead before the wedding. Today, a visit to the doctor and your new home. Then, talking to the priest, packing, moving, trying on your gown," Luca ticked off each one on his fingers as he leaned nonchalantly against the door frame. His gaze lingered on her face for several long seconds before Luca pushed away to stalk forward. He leaned down to capture her lips in a sizzling kiss before whisking her bedcovers away.

Quickly, Carina pulled the hem of her shirt down her thighs to hide herself. Her mind dealt first with being exposed before she could focus on his words. "What do you mean, doctor? I'm not sick."

"And, I'm going to keep you that way." He tugged her out of bed and whisked her nightshirt over her head.

"Hey," she protested, covering her body with her hands. In the bright light of the morning, she felt much more exposed than she had last night.

"None of that, Little girl. I don't want to give you a reminder spanking. No hiding from Daddy," Luca corrected sternly as he encircled her wrists with his fingers. Pulling them away, he pressed them firmly to her sides. When she stayed in that position, he leaned forward to kiss her lightly.

"Go potty while Daddy picks out something for you to wear."

Grateful she could have a bit of privacy, Carina ran to the restroom. After using the toilet, she looked at herself in the mirror. Wide brown eyes looked back at her. "I don't know what's going on," Carina whispered to herself before washing her hands and splashing water on her face. She hesitated at the door.

"Carina, come see what I've picked out for you to wear." Luca's voice held an undercurrent of impatience.

She peeked into the room and saw him standing next to the freshly made bed. His back was to her, allowing Carina to scan his hard body. While Luca seemed to have great genetics thanks to his silver fox father, he obviously stayed fit and active. She wondered what he did to work out.

As if he could feel her eyes on his body, Luca turned. "Come, Carina. I do not wish to be late for your appointment." Stepping forward, he held out a hand and drew her forward.

Her eyes traced over the simple cotton dress and panties on the bed. "I'll need a bra, too," she turned to grab one from the dresser.

"No, Carina. I've picked out what I want you to wear.

When we are alone, there is no need for big girl items of clothing. Only when we have to pretend with others will you where those clothes that the niceties of society. Last night, big girl clothes. Today, Little girl."

"I can't go out without a bra," she protested.

"Of course, you can. When I shop for you next, I'll consider some supportive camisoles."

While she was pondering that, Luca settled the dress over her bare skin. Automatically, she moved to thread her arms through the short sleeves. Carina also stepped into her panties as he held them out, bracing herself with a hand on his broad shoulders. Loving the feel of his muscles bulging under her fingers, Carina tried not to give her attraction to him away. Luca's sizzling wink as he guided the panties into place let her know that he could feel the heat gathering between her thighs. Carina looked down to hide what must be a bright red blush as her cheeks heated.

Chuckling, Luca simply took her hand and led her down the hallway. At the bathroom, she hesitated. "It won't take me a minute to put on some makeup," she rushed to assure him.

"No makeup," he answered without slowing his pace. When she looked back over her shoulder at her tidied bed, Daffy looked back at her. Suddenly, she craved the reassurance of her stuffie.

"Can I take Daffy?"

That question brought him to a standstill. He looked back at the yellow kitten he'd placed in the position of honor on the center pillow. "I think Daffy should certainly come with us." Luca released her hand and allowed Carina to run down the hall to scoop up her stuffie. Extending his palm to her, he squeezed her fingers as she rejoined him. "You please me, Little girl."

Luca ushered her into the plush sedan claiming the center of her driveway. Flustered when he leaned across her in the small area, she fumbled with the seatbelt as she inhaled his potent masculine scent. His wide shoulders swallowed up most of the room. "Allow me, Carina," he instructed as he brushed her hands away from fastening the seatbelt.

"I can do it, Luca," she rushed to reassure him.

"Not any longer." With a light kiss, Luca withdrew.

She watched him circle the front of the car. He moved as he always had—smooth and confident. Even in the eighth grade when everyone was awkward and dealing with pimples, Luca had controlled everyone around him. His suave manners and old-world charm worked magically on everyone from twelve-year-olds to the principal. He watched her like a jungle cat stalked its prey. Carina's heart pulsed faster as she fully woke up and digested everything that had already happened that morning.

"I don't need to go to the doctor," Carina rushed to tell him again.

"Little girl, you need to leave these important things to your Daddy to handle," Luca warned as he started the car and began to reverse it.

"Surely, you aren't going to take this... this fetish, so far."

The car stopped and Luca shifted it into park before turning to look at her. "Your life has changed, Carina. The minute you returned that card to me, you lost control of everything. I am giving you a bit of grace because I know you are scared. You have a chance to live out your most private fantasies. Will you be brave enough to enjoy them?" His hand reached forward to brush over Daffy's soft fluff.

"Are you going to hurt me?" she whispered.

"I will punish you when you are naughty."

"How bad?"

"That will depend on your behavior, Little girl. You will earn rewards as well as punishments. Now, you have to decide. Are you going to be good or bad?" Luca nodded at the elderly woman who lived next door. She hovered on her

25

front stoop, looking curiously toward the handsome visitor in the expensive vehicle.

"I don't want to be spanked again," she announced.

"Then, we're off." Luca set the car in reverse and backed out of the driveway as if she had conceded everything.

Soon, he pulled into a parking lot of a nondescript glass and steel office building. Driving to the far, right-hand side of the building, he waved a card at a sensor and opened a gate into a smaller parking area. Carina twisted to look back as the gate closed behind them. She couldn't see the main parking lot that was filled with cars anymore.

"I will come help you out," Luca warned, placing a restraining hand over her knee when she automatically moved to unfasten her seat belt.

Instead of watching him round the car again, Carina glanced out the windows, trying to determine what type of business this was. Luca had mentioned a doctor. Could there be a medical office in this high rise?

"We're almost late for our appointment, Carina. We'll have to hurry." Luca tugged her from the car and wrapped an arm around her waist. He ushered her through a sliding glass door, proclaiming, Dr. Hendricks, private physician. Leading her to the receptionist at the front, Luca greeted the pleasant-looking woman, "Hi, Kelly. Carina is here for her introductory appointment. I hope you received her medical records from her previous doctor."

"Hi, Mr. Ricci. It's nice to meet you, Carina." The receptionist smiled gently at Carina who looked back and forth between them uncertainly. "We did get Carina's records and Dr. Hendricks is reviewing them right now."

A nurse in colorful scrubs arrived at the front desk. "Mr. Ricci, the doctor is ready to see Carina now. Please bring her back to examination room three."

With Luca's arm wrapped around her waist, he steered her down the hallway. When she hesitated when the nurse opened the door, she winced as his fingers closed painfully on her side. Bucking forward, she scooted into the exam room and stopped against to stare at the man in the white coat.

"Carina, this is Dr. Hendricks. He's going to be your new doctor."

"Hi, Dr. Hendrick. I'm glad to meet you," she answered politely before adding, "I've always gone to Dr. Roberts."

"Yes, Mitchell Roberts is a very good physician. He was sorry to see you change practices but understood you needed specialized care. Come in and sit down with your Daddy. Who is this with you today?" he asked, waving a hand toward the stuffy she crushed against her chest.

"Daffy," she whispered. "It's short for Daffodil."

"I'm glad you brought a friend, Daffy is welcome any time." He waved a hand at the chairs at the side of the room and waited for them to sit. "You understand that your Daddy has brought you to me to take care of as a Little girl should be. Immediately, we will make some changes to support you. It is important that you always tell me the truth, Carina. Can I count on you?"

"Y... yes," she whispered in a stuttering voice. She didn't know what it was about this doctor that commanded obedience, but she couldn't imagine not doing what the handsome doctor said. When Luca rubbed her back to encourage her, Carina scooted a bit closer to his warmth.

"I'm going to ask you some big girl questions before I do my exam. First, do you have any health concerns?" he asked, watching her as the nurse prepared to type into the laptop.

"Um, I'm pretty healthy," she rushed to assure him.

"I'm glad to hear that, Carina. Let's start with the medicine you are on now. Dr. Roberts shared he has prescribed medicine for migraine headaches and for severe menstrual cramps. Is there any other medicines or drugs that you take?"

"Oh, I don't take those all the time. Just every once in a while." She rushed to add, "I don't take any illegal drugs."

"I'm glad. Where do your migraine headaches hurt worse?" he asked and paused for her to lift her hand to indicate over her eyes and top of her head. "Anything else, I should know about your health?"

Carina shook her head quickly. Maybe this wouldn't be so bad.

"Perfect. Luca if you'll help Carina take off her clothes and sit on the exam table, I'll do a preliminary exam."

"Of course," Luca pulled her to her feet. "Let's put Daffy here," he suggested, tugging the kitten from her hands.

"You don't have to stay in here," she whispered furiously.

"I will be with you for all your appointments, Little girl." His hands lifted her dress and she frantically held the material over her thighs.

"Luca, no. I don't need an exam!"

"I will step out to gather a few supplies for you, Luca," Dr. Hendricks spoke calmly. He was not disturbed by Carina's struggles to resist.

When the door clicked quietly behind him, Luca turned her quickly over the exam table and ripped her dress up to her waist. The sound of the material actually tearing made her freeze in place. When she felt her panties pulled down to her ankles, Carina began to struggle in earnest.

Whack! Whack! Whack! Her spanking last night seemed almost light in comparison to the heavy swats of Luca's big hand. Making it even worse, he said absolutely nothing—just continued to spank her already sore bottom.

Instantly tears poured from her eyes. "Luca, no! You can't just beat me if I don't do what you say!" She tried to be strong and stand up despite his restraining hand between her shoulder blades.

"Someone's being naughty," a faint female voice reached

her ears through the wall that separated her exam room from another.

"Little girls have to learn the hard way to behave sometimes."

"I don't get spankings anymore."

"Not very often, sweetheart. Hopefully, the Little girl next door will figure out that Daddy is always in charge."

"I hope so. Then, she can be happy."

Carina looked over her shoulder at Luca. Pausing to rub her bottom, he watched her carefully with a very serious expression. "Everyone knows?"

"Everyone is here for the same reason you are. Every Little girl is lucky to have a Daddy who cares for them completely. Do you need more swats, or will you cooperate with the doctor?"

"No more," she pleaded, pulling Daffy over her eyes.

"Stand up. Let's get this dress off," he directed evenly. His breath and demeanor under total control. Spanking her hadn't stressed him at all.

As she stood to allow him to take off the torn dress, Carina realized that in Luca's mind, this was ordinary. She didn't follow directions. She was disciplined. He'd even found a doctor who treated Little girls. Instantly, she felt her resistance evaporate. This was what she'd always dreamed of —having a Daddy. Being Little. *Can I do this?*

"Sounds like Carina is ready for her exam," the doctor's voice announced as he walked back in with an armful of supplies. "Luca, we'll see what you need for Carina's care. You may have already equipped her nursery."

"I have a few things, doctor, but I'm eager to see what you recommend."

Carina stood nude in the bright light as the two men talked casually about her. She lifted Daffy to cover her face. Thank goodness her Daddy had allowed her to bring the stuffie!

29

"Step up on the scale, Carina," the doctor instructed.

Reassured by this familiar step, Carina followed his directions. With her height and weight recorded, she swallowed hard at his next words.

"Lie on your tummy."

She watched him pull on the first glove before scrambling to follow as Luca cupped a hand over her fiery bottom. Trying not to flash her intimate areas to the men, Carina sat down and then rolled over on her stomach. She buried her face against the cool padding. Swallowing hard as she felt her buttocks separated, Carina exhaled audibly as the thick thermometer slid coldly inside her body.

"Good girl," Luca praised. He stood next to the exam table and stroked his fingers through her hair as time tickled slowly by.

Finally, the doctor removed it and patted her bottom softly. "Sit up, Carina."

Luca helped her turn over and sit at the edge of the table> She could feel the slippery lubricant between her buttocks. Shifting restlessly, Carina watched the doctor record her temperature and place the thermometer on a tray of supplies. She swallowed hard at the sight of two speculums and a variety of other things she didn't recognize.

After changing gloves, the doctor checked her eyes, ears and throat. He had her read from a chart and a small card. After looking at her thoughtfully, Dr. Hendricks asked, "Do you get headaches often after reading?"

"Usually after grading and planning my lessons," she answered before tears gathered in her eyes at the thought of someone else leading her class. She was going to miss teaching so much.

"Have you ever worn glasses or contacts?"

"No. I see very well," she answered, puzzled.

"Luca, I think it would be wise to have Carina's eyes examined."

"I will make the appointment. Do you have anyone you recommend?" he asked.

"Yes. I'll give you his information. Okay, Little girl. Lie back on the table."

Once in position, Carina closed her eyes as Dr. Hendricks examined her breasts thoroughly. His fingers assessed her sensitive breast tissue. She never did this at home like you were supposed to. It scared her to feel all the lumps and bumps. When he pinched her erect nipples, she opened her eyes in surprise.

"Perfectly healthy. I would guess you never perform self-examinations." When she shook her head, Dr. Hendricks patted her shoulder. "Luca, you'll need to check her breasts on a regular schedule. After her period is a good time to see if anything feels different to you."

When Luca nodded, the doctor moved his hands down to her stomach and began to press in different places. "Do you have any trouble going to the bathroom, Carina?"

Her mind instantly flashed to Luca's announcement that he would give her enemas. She rushed to reassure both men, "I'm fine. I don't have any stomach problems."

"A maintenance program of bottom treatments will keep Carina feeling well," he commented to Luca before adding, "Help me move your Little girl into position." Dr. Hendricks tilted the stirrup into place and lifted her leg to fit her foot into place. Luca followed his example.

"I've already had my PAP this year," she rushed to assure the doctor.

He just patted her thigh. "Scoot down to the edge of the table, Carina. That's it. Good job," he complimented as she automatically followed the instructions. He seated himself on a low stool between her thighs.

Swallowing hard, Carina stared up at the ceiling. She hated these exams so much. Her eyelids flew open at the touch of Luca's hand. He interlaced his warm fingers with hers and squeezed. Searching his face, she saw a hint of the young man who'd captivated her so many years ago. She hadn't held on to that card for so many years because of his powerful family. Luca had chosen her.

Now there was no debate that he was in complete charge, but a bit of emotion she'd sensed behind his carefully developed persona so many years ago peeked out again. He had chosen her for a reason. Luca didn't make mistakes. He knew her inner thoughts and desires. She squeezed his hand in response.

Dr. Hendricks's light shone warmly on her inner thighs. Carina felt his gloved hand stroke down her inner thigh, and she closed her eyes. Luca was there. He'd take care of her.

The doctor's touch was thorough. He did not rush through the exam but deliberately examined her body. Carina tried not to respond as his fingers glided over her clitoris and outer lips. One thick finger slid inside her body and rotated to slowly feel the interior walls. When he removed it, she knew what must be coming next.

"You'll feel the speculum, Carina," Dr. Hendricks announced.

She shivered slightly at the feel of the metal. It wasn't ice cold or even cool as she'd felt before. Just that little bit of reassurance that the doctor was concerned about her comfort made her relax slightly. Carina felt that stroking hand again on her inner thigh.

"Little girls don't like to go to the doctor, Carina. I try to take care of my patients," the doctor said softly.

"Thank you," she whispered.

A clicking sound resounded loudly through the exam room as he opened the device inside her vagina. She could feel the heat of the light move slightly as he focused it on her interior walls. The familiar poke of the swabs followed before Dr. Hendricks spoke again.

"Luca, Carina's body is very narrow. She is not a virgin

but has not had very much experience." He continued, ignoring the soft gasp from Carina's lips, "You will need to use a significant amount of lubricant in the beginning to avoid tearing her entrance. I will send home with you some healing cream to use twelve hours or so after sex. It will soothe her."

"Can the cream be used rectally as well?" Luca asked.

There was no emotion or stress in his voice. It was as if he were asking whether she could use eyedrops. Carina tightened her hold on Luca's hand, silently begging him to stop asking such embarrassing questions.

"Yes. That's the next step in my exam." Dr. Hendricks released the device and allowed it to slide from her body. "You'll feel my finger first, Little girl."

Carina curled up slightly from the table. Instantly, Luca released her hand to press her to the table. He reached over her body to grab a wide strap she hadn't noticed. Quickly, he stretched it over her ribcage pinning her in place. With a snap, the metal fastener proclaimed her secure.

"Luca, no!" she begged.

Luca retook her hand and held it firmly in his. "Take some deep breaths and blow them out, Little girl. Dr. Hendricks will be done soon."

"But, Luca!" Carina protested as the doctor stood between her legs to press on her abdomen. She closed her eyes as he inserted a finger in her vagina as well as her rectum. *Please let this be over soon!*

Dr. Hendricks removed his fingers and settled on his stool once again. "You're doing very well, Carina," he praised.

Hearing the click of metal once again, Carina tightened her buttocks. She knew where that smaller speculum was going. "Owww!" she howled as he inserted it and opened it several clicks.

"Deep breaths, Little girl." The doctor's calm voice reassured her. She'd always been one to respect authority. He wasn't concerned in the least.

Again, she felt the tickle of swabs inside her. Squirming her hips without thinking, she gasped as warmth blossomed inside her. "It burns!" she urgently whispered.

"Just a bit of medicine—The heat will fade. I promise," Dr. Hendricks spoke as he continued to apply the warming solution to the walls of her rectum.

"Luca, Carina need to have a thorough bottom cleaning and rinse. I had figured as a teacher, she would have some chronic constipation issues. That is definitely true. She also is dehydrated from not drinking enough liquids."

Turning to Carina, he asked, "Do you prefer milkshakes or lemonade?"

"Milkshakes have too many calories," she blurted and then looked back at Luca to make sure he didn't think she was heavy. Carina automatically pulled her stomach in.

"Perhaps a few of both would be best, doctor. Carina can see which she prefers. How many glasses or bottles a day would you like her to drink?"

"At least eight, but 10 would be better."

"I'll start monitoring her liquid intake. And after her enema, how often would you suggest to maintain her health?"

Looking up at him, Carina tried to use her facial expression to signal him that she wasn't going to put up with that. Anger flared through her as he released her hand to press in various spots on her stomach without reacting at all to her silent message. It really pissed her off that each place he touched actually didn't feel good. *The doctor couldn't be right!*

"At least once a week for the first month. Then bring her back for a check up on her progress." Dr. Hendrick stripped off his gloves. Was it over? "Many young women suffer from difficult menstrual cramps. I'm going to send home with you a bit stronger medicine in suppository form for you to administer two days before her cycle begins and two days after. She'll be groggy those 5 days of the month but Carina will be much happier."

"Thank you, doctor," she whispered. He did seem to care about how she felt and was going to help her. Maybe Dr. Hendricks knew what he was doing?

"Luca, come caress Carina to orgasm."

"What? What kind of exam is this?" Carina's train of thought completely derailed at the doctor's statement. She moved on the table trying to free herself from the bonds and supports that held her firm against the table.

Luca wrapped a squeezing hand around her shoulder to restrain her as the doctor continued without acknowledging her efforts, "I'd like to see how she reacts. Her body responded very well to her exam today."

"Nooo! No, Luca!" she begged.

Leaning over her body, Luca kissed her softly before pressing his lips to the swell of her sensitive underside of her breast. "Mmm. You taste sweet, Little girl," he praised. When her gaze flashed to Dr. Hendricks who shifted to lean against the counter, he added, "Focus on me, Carina."

She locked her eyes on his face. Lifting her hands to hold on to his shoulders, Carina blocked out the view of the doctor to center her attention on him. His lips tasted her body and she realized he'd never caressed her body. Last night, his touch had been a quick orgasm to console her after her spanking. His skills last night had astounded her but now she understood why all the older, female students back in school had flocked to him.

Luca took his time. He wrapped his tongue around her nipple to tease it before sucking it strongly into his mouth. The discrepancy between fast and slow captured her attention. What would his next touch be like?

She sucked her stomach in as his fingers trailed down her abdomen. Luca pressed kisses to the valley between her breasts before repeating the process to her right breast. Just as his mouth captured her nipple, Luca slid his fingers into the slick juices between her thighs. Retracing the doctor's clinical touch, he overwrote her memories with tingling pleasure.

Softly moaning when his thick finger entered her, Carina lifted her pelvis as much as possible. She bit her lip as the mixture inside her bottom continued to warm. The combination of Luca's mouth nibbling across her sensitive breasts, the heat filling her, and his wicked fingers made her beg, "Please, Luca. Please!"

"Come, Little girl. Let me feel your pleasure. Soon, I will fill you with my cock inside of my fingers."

That promise growled in Luca's deep voice pushed her over the edge. Mewing in pleasure, Carina squirmed on the table trying to get closer to him. He captured her lips, silencing Carina with a possessive kiss as his fingers continued to play between her legs. Luca held her in place with the weight of her torso making her take everything he gave. When she collapsed, boneless on the exam table, those fingers calmed and his kisses softened.

Finally, he stood up next to her. Lifting his fingers to his mouth, Luca tasted her flavor. "Sweet, Little girl. I think I'm addicted to your taste." She could feel her face heat with embarrassment when the doctor shifted. How had she forgotten him observing everything?

"Good reactions. I think you have chosen your Little well," Dr. Hendricks remarked. Before turning to make a note in her file. He unwrapped a package and retook his place between her splayed legs.

"A little medicine to treat your bottom," he announced and quickly pushed a suppository into her bottom, making her clench her buttocks tightly from the last orgasmic spasms ricocheted through her body. It was followed by a slender plug.

Instantly the warming sensation began to fade. To Carina's horror, she realized that she missed it. "Oh!"

Dr. Hendricks patted her thigh. "I know Little girl. It's hard to leave the doctor's office somedays. Your Daddy will take you home to treat you with some special medicine. I think you'll enjoy it."

"Medicine?" she echoed, looking back at Luca.

The two men just chuckled and unfastened her bindings. Luca slide a hand under her back to help Carina sit up. She swayed slightly as the room moved around her. Without thinking, she leaned against Luca's strength. As they talked, her mind whirled. How had that happened? It sounded like Luca planned on bringing her here regularly. When the doctor took her arm gently, she opened her eyes, allowing him to push the thoughts from her brain.

"I'm going to run some tests, Carina. Hide your head against your Daddy," he instructed as he wrapped a rubber tourniquet around her upper arm. A quick stick and he was finished.

"Would you like Carina to be on birth control?" the doctor asked Luca directly.

"Yes."

"Our pharmacy here can fill that. Check with the nurse to pick it up as you leave. Use protection for the first two weeks. Luca, you will need to take charge of this. Littles often forget."

"Definitely," Luca agreed.

"Here's a container for a urine specimen. Use the cleansing wipes before allowing Carina to fill the cup." He set the plastic beaker on the counter. "Carina, it was lovely to meet you. No spanking next time, Little girl."

With that warning, the doctor disappeared out of the door. Carina jumped as Luca pushed her thighs apart. Automatically, she tried to bring them together. Anticipating this, he had stepped between her knees to block her with his body. As she watched, Luca tore a packet of a small premoistened towelette. When he started to clean her skin, Carina reached for the white square.

"I can do it."

"No."

His hands continued to wipe her juices from her inner thighs. Pitching that one away on to the rumpled paper lining the exam table behind her, he reached for another packet and opened it. This time, he slid the cold wipe along her inner folds. Carina gasped at the chilly shock to her most intimate area.

"Cold, isn't it? Just one more and we'll be done. Hold on to my shoulders if you need to," he suggested.

Glad to have something to do, Carina wrapped her fingers around his muscles. She closed her eyes as he took the last wipe and took his time to clean carefully around her urethra. Finally, he leaned to the counter and picked up the specimen container.

"Let's go to the potty, Little girl. You don't want to have an accident." Luca opened a door to a small room with a toilet. He helped her sit down and then opened the jar before leaning forward to hold it to her body.

"I can do it!" She rushed to take it from his hands, but her body reacted immediately to being seated. Embarrassed, she hid her face against his shoulder. The feel of a soft kiss against her hair made her smile. She was beginning to learn. This was Luca. He would demand to take care of her, but underneath his powerful demeanor lurked something —tender.

CHAPTER 4

Redressed in the torn dress, Carina clung to Luca's hand as he escorted her through the office with the doctor's supplies and her new prescription. She gasped at the renewed sting on her punished bottom as her Daddy helped her and Daffy back into the car. Carina tried to ignore the sack of supplies that Luca had placed in the back seat, but she could see it if she turned her head just a fraction. Studiously looking ahead, she asked, "Where are we going? I need to change my dress."

"I'm taking you to my home. I have clothes for you in the nursery."

"The nursery?"

"Yes, Little girl."

He turned a corner and the paper bag in the back seat crashed over. Automatically, she glanced back when she heard the noise. A large container of thick, bullet-shaped items rolled on the leather. A pink box drew her attention. The label was partially blocked by black zippered case. She could read ene... ba... Carina whipped around to face the front.

"You aren't going to use that stuff, right?" she asked, focusing on the traffic in front of the car.

"Yes. Whatever Dr. Hendricks prescribes to keep you healthy."

"Luca, you can't really…"

"Daddy, Carina. Call me, Daddy."

Swallowing hard, Carina didn't like his answer. Could she really give him this much control? When his hand covered her trembling knee, Carina looked over at him. Luca maneuvered through the heavy traffic with quiet confidence. Just as he did everything in life, Luca projected self-assurance.

No, that wasn't right. He was in total control. Now, he was in total control of her. She hugged Daffy tightly to her chest as thoughts whirled inside her mind. "I'm scared," she whispered.

Luca lifted one hand from the steering wheel to wrap around her knee. He squeezed lightly. "Thank you for telling your Daddy. What frightens you?" Steering off the highway, he pulled into a busy parking lot and into an empty space at the far side.

"I don't know that I can do this," she confessed.

"What frightens you?" he repeated. "Are you worried about how I'll take care of you or how you'll respond?"

"What?" Aghast, Carina looked at him as she tried to make sense of his words. Could he be right?

"Giving up your power is overwhelming. Allowing your fantasies to come true is even more unsettling—at least at first."

She studied his face, trying to read his emotions. He wasn't surprised by her reaction. "How do you know me so well?"

"You were the one I chose."

"That was a long time ago, Luca."

"Daddy."

"Okay…" she drew out the word to make a point. "That was a long time ago, Daddy."

The corners of his lips twitched upward before he schooled his expression. She had amused him. "A Ricci knows. I've only ever had one card. I chose you. I've been waiting for you."

"Really?" she squeaked. "I know you've dated other women."

"Of course. That was before you came to me."

"You're done with other women now?" she asked, skeptically.

"Yes."

He's telling the truth. She looked at him in amazement. Needing to solidify the facts, she asked, "You had only one card."

"Yes."

"Have you regretted giving it to me?"

"No."

"How long would you have waited?"

"Until you came to me."

"That could have been a long time," she asked, arching one eyebrow.

"Susana was just a convenient excuse."

"What?"

"I was not the only one keeping track of someone."

Her searches online and the many times she'd asked others casually about him—he didn't know, did he? She stared at him. While his composed face didn't give away his thoughts, she whispered, "You do know."

"Yes. I could wait for you to come to me, Little girl, for a few years. My patience was coming to an end."

She dropped her eyes down to the soft kitten in her arms. Carina wanted to be angry or upset that he had tracked her so thoroughly. Instead, she found it thrilling. The brainiac she had been as a teenager should have been the last type of person that Luca would choose. He'd never waivered from his decision. His sights had always been focused on her.

The hand on her knee moved, smoothing over her flesh. He squeezed her knee slightly. "It's okay, Little girl. We're together now and I won't let you go."

That statement could have scared her more, but it didn't. Carina peeked up at Luca. "I don't know how to be a Little girl," she confessed.

"It's okay. I know how to be a Daddy."

"O… Okay," She stumbled over the small word that ceded her care to him.

Luca leaned forward to cup her face. Guiding her lips to his, he kissed her softly and then again with irresistible skill. She loved his kisses. Her Daddy knew how to use his lips. Carina opened her mouth under his, silently asking for more.

Honk! A loud car horn interrupted the sensual bubble wrapped around them. Luca lifted his head and slowly turned to look at the rearview mirror at the carload of teenage boys making kissy faces at him. She couldn't help herself. Giggles burst from her lips. The built-up tension inside the sedan evaporated.

"Come on, Little girl. I need to get you alone," Luca growled, putting the car in reverse and moving backward. The car behind him zipped away as if he'd willed it to get lost. Within moments, they were back on the highway.

This time as she squeezed Daffy to her chest, humor motivated her rather than fear. Carina relaxed against the leather seat. *Luca, er Daddy, will take care of everything.*

She watched the city fade away into the suburbs. She recognized the area. It wasn't too far from where she'd lived as a child. Luca turned down a wide driveway and paused as the gate opened silently ahead of them obviously signaled by their approach. After negotiating a curve in the drive lined by huge trees, an enormous house appeared before them.

This was definitely not the upper middle class home she had lived in growing up.

"This is your house?" she asked, leaning forward to peer at the magnificent building more closely.

"My family home, yes. I built a wing off the main house six years ago. It is convenient for our business to be together. The estate is secure, and we have our own space."

"We?"

"Yes, Little girl. You and I. I designed our home for us."

"We're going to live with your parents?"

"No, Carina. I don't see my parents often. Watch," he paused at a fork in the road. "If we continue, we'll approach the front entrance. That is the original house where my parents live and entertain. We are going to our wing." He turned to the left and circled the side of the building. As the car swung around, she saw a new addition modeled with the same majestic style and old world charm. A large porte-cochere welcomed Luca to drive under the covered entrance. Immediately, a well-dressed man emerged from the large wooden double doors as Luca parked the car.

"Brian, would you put the car in the garage for me?" he asked upon exiting the car.

"Of course," the man with a hint of gray in his hair replied with a smile. "Is this your Carina?"

Luca opened the door and released Carina's seatbelt. She had almost unfastened it herself but stopped at the last moment. His light peck on her forehead should not have thrilled her as much as it did. Carina realized with a start that she wanted to please him. Stepping out of the car with his assistance, she smiled at the man before her as she moved Daffy to her side out of sight.

"I am Carina," she assured him.

"What a beautiful Little girl, you are. Welcome to your new home."

"Little girl?" she echoed as she tried not to panic.

"There are no secrets here. Brian has been with our family for many years. He will protect you as I would," Luca explained, putting an arm around her waist to guide her into the house. "Brian, Dr. Henricks sent home some supplies. Would you bring those in for us?"

"Of course." He smiled kindly at Carina before sliding in behind the wheel.

"Come, Little one. I would like to show you our house." He opened the door and ushered her through. Inside, a giant foyer greeted them. A door sat open to the right of the entrance. "This is Brian's office. If he is not here, you can reach him by picking up this phone and pressing the gray button. It connects to the cell phone he always carries —day or night. If you need to reach me, I am the first button, red."

"On all the phones?" she asked, curiously. Built in phones were so outdated. This seemed very convenient but old-fashioned.

"Press red on any phone and it will forward you to my cell phone. Try it," he urged, gesturing to the phone.

"Really?" When he nodded, she picked up the ornate receiver and pressed the red button. Instantly, his phone sounded from his pocket. "Hang up and press gray."

"Hello, this is Brian. How can I help you?" The pleasant tones of the butler greeted her.

Luca plucked the phone from her hand and spoke, "Thank you, Brian. Just giving Carina a tour and explaining how to get in touch with everyone." He hung up the phone after saying goodbye.

"What are the other colors?" She asked as she followed him into the house.

"The kitchen, my father in the other wing, the garage," he answered off-hand. "Here is our entertainment space if we have visitors."

Carina looked around the beautifully decorated space and

mentally counted chairs. You could entertain a huge crowd here. "Are we going to have a lot of parties?"

"No. This space exists solely to keep our private and public areas separated."

"Can I see our space?" she asked.

"Next on our tour," he answered. Leading her back into the foyer, he gestured to closed doors ahead. Taking her hand, he tugged her forward to escort her through the right door. "Here are our rooms. The TV room," he paused to let her look around the inviting space featuring a large TV and a heavily cushioned sectional.

"Here's Daddy's room," he pointed out as they passed a room decorated in a brown and tan color scheme. It looked very masculine.

"This is your nursery, Carina. Tell me what you like and don't like."

Carina turned in all directions, trying to take in the room. All those books she'd read had talked about nurseries. She'd thought they must not really exist for adults. She was wrong.

The walls were painted lemon yellow. It was bright and cheerful. Squeezing Daffy, she realized her stuffie almost matched. She didn't know what to look at first. There was a quiet space to the right with an oversized rocker and a table. A bottle filled with a milky white substance sat at the ready.

Noting all the adult-sized furniture, she realized that she would fit comfortably into them. Draped with flowing fabric from above, the bed fit for a princess displayed fluffy white and yellow bedding. A thick quilt was turned back to welcome someone to climb in and rest. After looking at Luca for permission, she walked toward it. Tentatively, she ran her fingers over the soft fabric. Set high above the floor, she would need help to climb up into it.

Luca walked up behind her and wrapped his arms around her waist. Pulling her tightly back against his hard body, he said softly, "Bottle and a nap for you, Little girl."

"I'm not really a baby," she protested.

"Here, you are." Leaning over, Luca scooped her into arms and carried her toward the waiting rocking chair.

She opened her mouth to assure him she could walk. Carina definitely wasn't used to being carried. The soft kiss on her forehead made her stay quiet. She liked this side of Luca—the nurturing, gentler side. He couldn't ever be des ed as soft. Not in a million years would anyone make that mistake. Squeezing Daffy in her arms, Carina held her breath in anticipation.

Lowering them smoothly to the chair, Luca balanced her on one knee. "Stand up for a minute. It's time to take this torn dress off, Little girl," he instructed. Wiggling the fabric up over her hips as she rose to her feet, Luca lifted it over her head and dropped it forgotten to the ground.

"I can't wander around in just my panties," she protested, hugging Daffy to her chest. At his stern look, she closed her mouth with a snap and allowed him to guide her back down onto her lap. She shifted restlessly for several seconds trying to find a comfortable spot that didn't stress her sore bottom.

"Try this, Little one." Luca brushed the nipple next to her lips.

When she opened her mouth to tell him she wasn't a baby, Carina discovered Luca had fast reflexes. The droplets of liquid that landed on her tongue tasted sweet. Swallowing, she couldn't help but murmur her appreciation, "Mmm!" Carina quickly decided since she was thirsty, it was okay to drink. She wiggled just a bit more to settle fully against his arm.

Without comment, Luca set the rocker in motion. It glided smoothly under them, lulling her even more into a feeling of contentment. Looking up at his handsome face, Carina met his eyes. His expression made her pause in drinking for a few seconds. Fiery passion reflected in his eyes. He wanted her here—exactly like this.

Something clicked into place inside her. They fit together perfectly. He wanted her just as she had always fantasized about living. Luca would never be a push over or a lenient Daddy. It would be his way or punishment. She would need to learn to give him the control he demanded.

The motion and the warm drink combined with the stress of her morning to make her sleepy. Her eyes blinked heavily. Carina tried to stay awake. She didn't want to miss any of this special time with Luca. No, with my Daddy, she corrected herself.

"Sleep, Little one. Nothing here will disappear," he promised. When she finished the bottle with a soft sucking sound, Luca removed it from her mouth and set it aside. His free hand stroked through her hair.

Treasuring his caresses, Carina stopped fighting to keep her heavy eyelids open. She snuggled a bit closer to Luca and focused on the delight of being held by this handsome man. His muscular warmth radiated against her like her own heat source.

Carina shifted a bit restlessly as he stood and carried her to the waiting bed. Unable to wake herself fully, she settled with a contented sigh into the soft bedding. With her bedraggled kitten tucked under her chin, she fell asleep.

CHAPTER 5

W aking in the beautiful bed, Carina pushed herself up on one arm to look around as rubbed the sleep from her eyes. She felt better. Heavens knows she hadn't slept well since returning that card to Luca. Carina always felt better if she got eight or nine hours of rest.

She looked over the edge of the bed and froze. It was so far down. Carina guessed that she could hop down but she'd never liked heights. A plush owl on the nightstand caught her attention. It was cute and cuddly but very straight as if stuffed with something rigid. Taking a chance, she cleared her throat.

"Daddy? I woke up. Could you come help me down?"

"I will be right there, Little girl."

His deep voice sent a shiver of delight down her spine. There wasn't much that she didn't like about Luca. Okay, everything was his way or not at all. She rubbed her bottom softly, feeling the residual heat from her spanking in the doctor's office. But her Daddy's dark, stern looks drew her. She shivered remembering his skilled mouth and fingers. The handsome man was definitely the lover she'd always fantasized about.

"Carina." His deep voice flowed over her like warm water. "You napped well." Luca leaned over to press a fiery kiss to her lips. When she lifted one hand to wrap around his neck to kiss him again, Luca removed it before pressing a soft peck to her palm. "Need to potty?"

Instant urgency to use the restroom made her squeeze her thighs together. "Yes, please!" she scooted a bit closer to the edge of the bed and looked over again. It was really far down there.

Carina looked up at Luca. "Could you help me?"

"Daddy."

"Could you help me, Daddy?" she corrected herself quickly.

Instantly, he whisked her from the covers and set her feet on the thick carpet. Taking her hand, Luca said, "Come with me." He led her quickly to the bathroom down the hall. Luca leaned over to tug her panties from her hips and help her step free. "Go potty."

Hesitating only a few seconds, the need to go overwhelmed her embarrassment. Carina dropped to the toilet. As she tinkled, she looked around the enormous room. There was an enormous, padded ottoman in the middle of the floor. "Who'd have a seat in the bathroom?" she wondered.

The rush of water from the sink drew her attention. As she finished, Carina looked to the side and noticed Luca was busy measuring a thick, milky solution into measuring cup. She quickly wiped herself dry and stood to flush the toilet.

Now standing, she could see a large rubber pouch bulging as the water gushed inside. The sink was huge and equipped with a tall faucet almost like you'd normally find in a kitchen. A supportive hook held the enema bag as Luca filled it. As she watched in horror, he added the white solution he'd measured into the container and suds began to burst over the sides. With a click, he shut off the water.

"All done?" When she nodded, he approached and took

her hand to lead her to the padded hassock. "It's time to treat your tummy. Move into position as you did for your spanking."

"I don't want this," she whispered, backing away from him.

"I know." He continued to pull her forward. When she stopped and leaned away to prevent him from towing her, Luca simply picked her up and carried her to the padded support. Placing her on her hands and knees, Luca held her in position with a firm hand between her shoulders and on her red bottom. He allowed her just enough freedom to twist slightly to the side to look at him.

"You will have an enema as Dr. Hendrick's prescribed. He is the expert. I will administer enemas frequently. You decide whether you want one today after being spanked with the naughty Little paddle," he paused to nod at the wall.

"You can't use that on me!" The words burst from her lips. Carina stared in horror at the large wooden rectangle with the words, Naughty Carina, engraved into it. The thick grooves from the letters would make the hard surface hurt even more. Next to the paddle hung another empty sturdy hook. *What hangs from that one?*

"It is your paddle. Only you can ask me to take it from the wall."

"I'm never going to ask for that."

"Oh, not with your words," he answered, "But, your actions will request correction. I can guarantee that. So, do you want to ask to be paddled or will you press your cheek to the ottoman?"

His hand pressed between her shoulders, urging her down. Carina looked fretfully back toward the waiting enema bag. The thick suds floated on the surface. "I don't want this, Luca. If I need to go to the bathroom, couldn't Dr. Hendricks prescribe some medicine."

"He has." Luca pressed steadily on her upper back.

Slowly, her arms yielded to his strength. Carina resisted at the last moment, but her chest collapsed to the cool surface. Immediately, she felt a wide band stretch across her upper back and snap into place under her other armpit. He fastened her hands before her With a few adjustments from Luca, she was tethered securely into place.

"Widen your legs, Little girl," he instructed, shifting her knee into a slight depression before wrapping a restraining strap over her calf. Quickly, Luca repeated the action on the other side. His hand patted raised Carina's bottom lightly. "Good job."

"Please, no, Luca!"

"I'll be right back," he promised.

Unable to slide flat to wiggle forward or back, Carina could only listen to his footsteps trailed away. A sloshing sound followed. She closed her eyes as tears welled in them. "I don't want this," she chanted repeatedly. Carina wanted him to know that she was not cooperating. He might be able to overpower her, but it wasn't right.

A sound behind her caused her eyes to flash open as he hung the solution-filled bag on the hook behind her. She could hear him adjusting something. The creak of hook as it adjusted to the weight echoed in her mind. Surely her body couldn't take all that.

"Luca! Please no!" she begged.

He caressed her displayed bottom tenderly. "I know this is hard, Carina. Daddies take care of their Littles intimately. It's my responsibility to make sure you feel better. Has your tummy been hurting?" he asked softly.

"No!"

"I don't believe you, Little girl. Think this time before you answer. At the party, you didn't eat anything. Your hand pressed repeated against your stomach. Dr. Hendricks and I can both feel your abdominal congestion. This isn't healthy."

"No, Luca. Please don't do this," she refused to entertain that he would be helping her.

"Daddy, Little girl. I am disappointed in you lying to me. There will be a consequence for that. Now, try to relax. You can make this easier on yourself."

The sound of a jar opening made her gasp. She tried to shift her hips as one of his hands separated her buttocks but the restraints kept her firmly in place. A cool substance touched that small, hidden entrance and she wailed as his finger slid inside her tight channel.

"Shh, it's okay, Carina. I'm here. I'm going to help you feel better."

He removed the invading digit and she felt flexible hose begin to slide into her body. Squirming desperately, she felt the restraints beginning to wear against her flesh. *Smack!* Carina froze in place.

"If I have to restrain you further, Valentine, you are not going to like it. Settle down or I will use the paddle before taking away the small amount of freedom you now have."

She exhaled audibly as the tubing continued to snake inside her. A sound of puffing air behind her was the only warning as it ballooned inside her.

"The tubing prevents any accidents, Little girl. You can relax and let the solution do its job." A snick sounded very loudly in the bathroom and warm liquid flowed inside her body. "If the pressure builds inside you, Carina, pant and it will ease. Your tummy is very congested. This first enema will be uncomfortable I'm afraid."

"First?" she wailed.

"I won't let your system get this clogged in the future."

"Please!" she begged.

The only response was a caressing hand over her bottom and down her spine. She could feel the warm fluid spurting through her body. "It stings!"

"That is the cleanser. The next one will feel better."

"You promise?" she clung to any hope of positives as her stomach began to swell. Panting desperately as her stomach began to hurt, she welcomed his hands rubbing softly over her abdomen to soothe the water deeper and ease the pressure.

Her desperate pleas to use the bathroom did not receive an answer. Luca stayed by her side, easing her discomfort. He was not, however, moveable from his objective. Carina sagged slightly in place. The control remained with her Daddy. She was powerless. Tears leaked from her eyes as he forced her to take the invasive treatment.

"It will be better, Valentine," he consoled her, wiping away the wet trails with a soft handkerchief.

Finally, she heard a gurgle and that click. "Is it over?"

"Not yet."

Carina heard the mechanical twisting of a dial. It sounded like her kitchen timer. "What's that?"

"Now your consequences add up. You lied to your Daddy and you injured yourself." He trailed the tip of one finger over the abrasions on her leg.

"Both are very bad decisions. Ten minutes for lying and five minutes for hurting yourself," he pronounced as he twisted the dial of a bright red object. With it set, Luca placed it directly in her view before taking a seat nearby chair.

"I have to wait fifteen minutes?" she wailed as her eyes shot daggers at the cartoonish tomato timer. The loud clicking just made it worse. It was so slow.

"Next time if you hurt yourself, the time will double to ten minutes. I will not allow anyone to injure you, Little girl —not even yourself."

Carina closed her eyes to block out the sight. She tried desperately to think of anything that could distract her. Her mind flashed back to one of those novels she had read over and over in the privacy of her room. That Little girl's Daddy had administered an enema to her as well. He'd followed it by… A creak of Luca's chair interrupted her thoughts.

She could hear his footsteps approach from behind her. Jostling forward when he stroked a warm hand over her buttocks and tugged gently on the hose to make sure it was secure. "Is it time?" she asked quickly, checking the timer to see that eight minutes remained on the device.

Without answer Luca trailed his fingers lower into the juices that had gathered between her thighs. She closed her eyes in shame, knowing that he knew all her secrets. He didn't comment or mock her but simply caressed her body with his expert skill. She responded immediately to his touch. The pressure of the water inside her body made the sensations feel doubled or tripled. Carina panted as she tried to hold off the orgasm that lurked so close.

"Come, Valentine," he commanded as he tweaked her clit.

Just as he demanded, Carina responded. Her body exploded into a frenzy of pleasure. His fingers never paused but continue to stroke and caress her. She screamed as a second wave of pleasure exploded as the first eased.

A loud buzzer sounded so close. Carina's eyes flew open to fix on that scarlet vegetable. The fifteen minutes were over. His wet fingers trailed down to her leg restraints and freed her. Quickly. he released her upper body as well and lifted her from the ottoman. Setting her feet on the tiled floor, he led her quickly to the toilet and released the tubing. She collapsed to the toilet to watch him gather the equipment for her second round.

"No more, Daddy," she pleaded.

"One more, Carina. You will feel better."

"I'm okay now," she rushed to assure him.

"One more, Carina."

CHAPTER 6

S itting at the table with Luca, Carina was ravenous. She squirmed in her chair as she looked over the delicious display in front of her. Everything looked so yummy!

"What would you like, Carina?"

"I can help myself."

"No, Little one. I will help you. These plates are heavy." Her stomach growled loudly as he paused. "How about a bit of everything? Then you can have more of your favorites?"

"Please," she requested. As she watched, he added a generous spoonful of the two salads and a half a sandwich of what appeared to be turkey and roast beef. When he set it down before her, she reached for one of the sandwiches before making herself wait for him to fill his plate.

"Eat, Carina."

"I don't want to be rude," she protested.

"You're hungry. We're alone here. Eat."

Immediately, she caved and picked up the turkey sandwich. Taking a huge bite, she hummed at the delicious taste. It wasn't like the simple sandwiches she fixed at home. This was laden with all types of additions: lettuce, tomato, even avocado.

"Good, huh?"

"I love avocado," she mumbled around her biteful, covering her hand over her mouth as politely as possible.

"I'll be sure to tell the kitchen that so they can have avocados on hand. I love them stuffed with seafood salad. Have you tried that?" Luca asked as he set a much more laden plate down in front of himself.

She watched him stab a fork into the broccoli salad and carry it to his mouth. Images of Luca's lips caressing her intimately burst into her mind. To her embarrassment, she felt her face heat and knew that he could tell the directions of her thoughts. Ripping her gaze away, Carina swallowed hard. As the food caught in her throat, she reached for the cup before her and took a large drink.

His chuckle brought her attention back to his face. "I'm glad you enjoy our playtime, sweet Valentine. I am looking forward to being buried deep inside you soon."

"Luca!" she said scandalized by his blunt language at the table.

"Daddy," he corrected automatically. "We are alone. Here we can speak confidentially. How is your tummy?"

Carina took time to sample the broccoli salad as well. This was one of her favorite concoctions. Again, she wiggled in her chair without planning to move. She considered his question as she chewed. Her stomach did feel better. Not wanting to encourage him, she swallowed and answered, "It's okay."

"I'll schedule in another cleaning tomorrow," he answered without missing a beat.

Looking at him in horror, she blurted, "It's better, okay? I don't need any more."

"If you are not sure that it made a significant difference, then Dr. Hendricks prescribed another round of treatment."

"Daddy, I'm great. My stomach feels much better. I didn't want to encourage you for the future. And..." she stopped wave a hand at the luncheon before them. "Is this really the time to have a discussion about this?"

"Yes. We are alone. No one else is here. I could wait and bring it up at our wedding reception if you'd prefer," Luca suggested with a raised eyebrow.

"You wouldn't!" she sputtered.

"In a group of Daddies and Littles, I wouldn't hesitate," he assured her before taking another bite of his sandwich.

Studying the expression on his face, Carina knew that was the truth. "I'm better. I didn't know how much it bothered me, but I feel much better now."

"Is this the truth?"

"Yes, Daddy. I'm telling you the truth," she answered urgently.

"Telling lies has consequences," he reminded her. When Carina nodded quickly, he changed the subject. "Eat, Little girl."

Immediately, she took another big bite of the delicious sandwich. The luxury of having a kitchen staff to prepare and present a luncheon when called was definitely not something she was used to enjoying. She peeked up at Luca's face to judge his mood. When he smiled at her, she asked, "Will we ever cook for ourselves?"

"Perhaps. I like cooking from time to time. Will you cook? No. You are not to use the stove if I am at work."

"Really?" she double checked. When he shook his head, she thought about being upset but then remembered she didn't like to cook much anyway. "Could we make cookies together sometimes? I like decorating them?"

"Cookie decorations, hmmm. I think I'd enjoy that as well," Luca said with a smile.

"It's a lot of fun," she rushed to assure him.

"I will ask the kitchen to stock our wing with the necessary ingredients. Do you like making the cookies or just decorating them?" he probed.

"Decorating them. Putting on the icing and the sprinkles is so much fun. I like eating them, too," she confessed.

"If they have icing and sprinkles, I think I would enjoy eating them as well. What else do you like to do, Carina?"

"I love to swim. I like flowers," she shared with a smile remembering the beautiful gardens that ringed the mansion.

"There is a pool in the backyard. Perhaps you'd like to take a walk in the gardens after lunch?"

"Don't you have to go to work? You can just drop me off at my apartment," she rushed to assure him.

"I often work from home, Carina. I checked in while you napped and will put in some hours this evening. Tomorrow, we will spend a bit of time in your apartment, boxing up anything of sentimental value. Starting today, I will keep you here with me."

"What happens to all my furniture?"

"It will be sold and the money placed in your bank account," he informed her casually.

"What if I don't want it sold?" she blustered.

"Then you can give it away to a charity or to friends. You will not need any furniture here. Again, if there is something special you wish to hold on to, you will tell me tomorrow and we will find space for it here."

Swallowing hard, she realized that she would stay with Luca forever now. She didn't need the furniture. Carina's gaze dropped to her lap and she traced one of the cute bunnies on the leggings that Luca had dressed her in before lunch. Her class would have loved these.

"Little one," Luca said gently. "Come sit on my lap." He scooted her chair away from the table and scooped her up onto his lap. Holding her close, he rocked her gently back and forth. When she sniffled, he hugged her a bit closer before leaning back to wipe her tears away with his cloth napkin. "It will be okay, Carina. There are just a lot of changes happening in your life all at the same time."

"It's so scary!" she whispered. "I don't have control of anything!"

"Perhaps that's a good thing. Maybe being in control is not all it's cracked up to be."

Her breath caught in her chest at that suggestion. Exhaling shakily, she thought about it. She'd had so many things to take care of: lesson plans, grading, parent contacts, meals, cleaning, shopping, bills. Carina had found it overwhelming frequently. How long had it been since she'd gotten to do something fun like decorate cookies?

"But adults have to do stuff," she whispered.

"Not all adults. Not you now."

"I can't just dump everything on you."

"Daddies are supposed to take care of all the big responsibilities. It's what we do. Our reward is having a Little to enjoy and cherish."

"You're not supposed to be nice. You're blackmailing me into marrying you."

"I made you a simple deal, Little one. You were not forced to accept. Now, the decision has been made. I hope you will allow yourself to enjoy our time together."

"But you just…" she began.

"And I'll continue to take care of you completely, Carina. You are my Little girl now."

Carina laid her cheek against his hard chest. "Do you think it will get easier?"

"Yes."

"Okay, Daddy." She peeked over her shoulder at his full plate.

"Try this potato salad, Carina. It's my favorite." He lifted his fork to scoop up a small bite from his plate. Holding it to her lips, Luca waited for her to open her mouth. When she did, he fed her.

"That's really good. It has bacon in it?" She asked sitting up to look over at her plate to see if he had given her some.

He had. Carina pushed her worries away. Her life was different—and so was he.

"Ready to go finish your lunch, Carina?"

"Yes," she agreed, allowing him to lift her back into her chair. Grabbing her fork, she took another bite of his favorite. Could it be better than the broccoli salad she loved? Maybe? Suddenly, she felt much better. Dashing away the last of the tears from her cheeks, she smiled at Luca. "Thanks."

"Any time, Valentine."

CHAPTER 7

W alking in the gardens was a delight. The variety of colors and types of flowers were more than she'd ever seen in someone's yard. Of course, there was a lot more land here to decorate. A man turned from a raise bed that he was working on to greet them.

"Hello, Master Luca. Is this your bride?"

"Samuel, the flowers are beautiful. Allow me to introduce, my Carina to you," Luca said proudly.

"Hi, Samuel," Carina chirped with a smile. "I love flowers."

"Hello, Miss Carina. I am very glad to meet you. And excited that you will enjoy the gardens. Is there a special flower that you love?" Samuel asked with a smile.

"I love the smell of gardenias. Do you have any in the garden?" she asked, looking around.

"There aren't any right now. But, there is a spot that would be perfect for gardenias. I will order them this afternoon."

"You don't have to do that. I'll just enjoy what's here," she rushed to assure him.

"Everyone has their favorites here. Do you see those pink roses on the corner there?" Samuel turned to point.

"Yes. Those are pretty."

"Of course, they are. Those are Master Luca's favorites. I put them in his room as often as possible. They are Carina roses. Now I understand why he loves them so much."

"Carina roses?" She turned to look at Luca. At his nod, she squeezed his hand in delight. "I'll have to go look at them closely."

Luca's phone rang in his pocket. "I'm sorry, Carina. This must be urgent or the office wouldn't interrupt me. May I leave you with Samuel for a couple of minutes?"

Quickly she nodded. She'd stay in the gardens forever if he'd let her. Luca moved a few yards away and answered his phone in a hushed voice. "I'll just get out of your hair and go see the roses," she suggested.

"Would you like to help me plant some new flowers?" Samuel asked, waving a hand toward the empty flower bed.

"Oh! I don't know a lot about planting things. I'd hate to mess up this beautiful place," she answered quickly as she stepped forward to see what he had lined up on the ledge.

"Then I will teach you. I always need an assistant who love flowers." Samuel insisted that she wear the space gloves he had in his supply basket. Then as Luca talked, Samuel coached Carina through planting a row of white lilies in the back of the raised bed. His fingers quickly straightened and adjusted her plants so that they all looked perfect when they'd finished.

"Those are beautiful, Samuel. What goes in front of them?" she asked eagerly.

"I could use your opinion. I have blue daisies and yellow daisies to go in front of the lilies. Which do you like better?" He held a small container of each up the white flowers.

"Could you do both? Maybe a clump of blue and then a clump of yellow?" she suggested hesitantly.

"I think that would look wonderful," a woman's voice said from behind her.

When Carina whirled around, she quickly greeted Luca's mother, "Hello, Mrs. Ricci. Please change my suggestion if there's something else you would like. Hi, Mr. Ricci."

"Please call me, Elizabeth or my favorite is Bethy while we are here at home," the older woman encouraged.

"Okay, Bethy." Carina answered cautiously. Luca's mom looked much different than she had at their previous meetings. Gone were her elegant gowns, makeup, and fancy upswept hairdo. Bethy wore jeans and a t-shirt with paw prints scattered at the bottom.

Carina glanced over at Luca who strode toward them. "You have a lovely home and garden," she said politely.

"It is your home now, too," Marco Ricci corrected her gently before adding, "I see Samuel has put you to work. What is it with Little girls and flowers?" he joked.

"Oh, he was just letting me help a bit while Luca was on the phone."

"Are you supposed to call him, Luca?" Bethy asked, tilting her head to look at Carina curiously.

"Bethy, she's nervous around us. We're strangers to her," Marco Ricci suggested softly.

"Hello, Father and Mother. How are you today?"

"Your mother woke up grumpy but has been much happier after her nap," Marco joked.

"I'm glad you're feeling better, Mother."

"Thank you," Bethy answered politely. "Can I help with the flowers?"

"Of course, you can. Here, Miss Bethy. Wear my gloves so your hands don't get dirty," Samuel quickly helped her put them on.

"Oh, I bet these were yours. You can wear these," Carina suggested, starting to take off the extra gloves from the gardener's basket.

"I like these. They're floppy," Bethy laughed waving the oversized gloves with a laugh. "Let's work on this together. It will be like a welcome home garden. A bit of you and me together," she suggested.

Immediately, Samuel put them to work. With his supervision, it didn't take long to have everything beautifully laid out. Both women stepped back to look at their handiwork.

"I love the clumps of color. That was an amazing suggestion, Carina. I think I'm going to like having you here," Bethy complimented with a smile.

"Thank you," Carina said, returning the smile. She'd had fun chatting with the much more relaxed woman. Mrs. Ricci had seemed somewhat distant at the social events.

"Come, Bethy. It's time for us to go in before you get too much sun." Marco appeared behind his wife to tug the gloves from her fingers before taking her hand.

"Okay, Daddy. I'll see you soon, Carina. I'd like to play again," Bethy called over her shoulder as they walked away.

"Daddy?" Carina whispered as Luca led her toward the pink roses she'd wanted to see closer.

"My mother has been my father's Little girl for thirty years. They are both very glad that you have come to join me now."

"They know I'm your Little girl?" she asked, appalled. Her mind wouldn't even process that Bethy was a Little girl as well.

"Yes."

"Isn't that strange?" she whispered as they came to a stop before the fragrant blossoms.

"It is what they both need and desire. How can I question them when I understand it myself so well?" he answered with honesty ringing from his words.

"That's how you knew in the eighth grade. Is that how you recognized me?" she asked staring at him.

"Yes. That's how I knew so many years ago that you were mine. What do you think of the Carina roses. They are very beautiful, just like you." He stopped to look back and forth between the roses and her face. "Your hair may just be a bit redder," he teased.

With her mind whirling, she allowed him to change the subject. "They are beautiful. I didn't know there were roses with my name." She leaned forward to sniff one blossom. "They smell so good."

"We will have them in our rooms tomorrow, I bet. Now, that you have charmed Samuel. I bet I will get to enjoy fresh flowers even more often. He delivers honeysuckle when it is in bloom to my mother's nursery himself."

"Samuel knows?" she asked before peeking back over her shoulder. He hadn't seemed to make fun of either of them.

"The staff here is familiar with our family. Most have been here for many years. They work hard to make us happy and are compensated for their loyalty. Come, Carina. I don't want you to burn either. Let's go inside and wash your hands. Then maybe you'd like to watch a movie while I finish some work?"

"That sound great… Daddy."

Her attempt to adjust to her new life was rewarded with a passionate kiss that curled her toes. When he stepped away, Carina followed him happily. Maybe this wasn't going to be so bad.

CHAPTER 8

"No, Daddy. I don't want that!" Carina cried out in distress. Stretched over Luca's knee, his forearm pinned her in place as he spread her buttocks.

He'd just bathed her tenderly in a large tub. The feel of his hands stroking the cleanser over her skin had been so arousing. She'd started to forget that she was powerless in this relationship and had enjoyed his attention. Those pleasant thoughts were wiped away as he trapped her over his lap.

"We will follow Dr. Hendrick's directions to keep you healthy. Two suppositories at night before the wedding and one or two each night after," he reminded her as he applied lubricant to that now exposed entrance. His finger slid inside to spread the slippery mixture on the walls of her tight channel.

"Please, no!" she begged. Feeling Luca removed his finger, she tensed waiting. A cold, rounded suppository touched her. She clenched her muscles with all her strength. Smack! Luca swatted her bottom distracting her. Her head reared back and she forgot to resist. Immediately, he pushed the medicine deep into her.

"One more, Little girl. Relax your bottom or I'll spank you again."

Carina did her best as she drooped over his thighs. He controls everything. Tears gathered in her eyes as he inserted the second, thick suppository. Clapping her hands over her eyes, she struggled not to cry. She didn't want him to know how helpless she felt.

Patting her bottom, Luca instructed, "Stand up, Little one. Let me clean my hands and then, it's time for your bottle and bed."

She stood forlornly by the rocking chair. Gripping the sides of her nightgown, Carina struggled not to give in to the temptation to run. She knew it wouldn't work. Luca had arranged everything. He controlled her life now. Carina turned her head to wipe her wet cheeks on the soft nightgown.

"Come here, Carina. Let me hold you." Luca picked up her rigid body and sat down. He cradled her gently against his chest as he rocked her. Stroking her red hair, Luca allowed the silence to wrap around them as he held her.

Unable to stop herself, Carina whispered, "I'm scared, Daddy."

"Facing your deepest desires and a tremendous amount of change at the same time would frighten anyone."

"Not you."

"Perhaps not, but we are talking about you. Drink, Little one. You need to be hydrated." He relaxed one arm to allow her to lie back. Brushing the nipple across her lips, he tempted her with the delicious formula she knew waited inside for her.

Gradually, she allowed her muscles to relax as she laid cradled in his arms. She was still mad but couldn't resist the allure of his tender treatment. Her eyelids felt very heavy. Carina blinked hard several times trying to ward off the sleepiness descending like a thick blanket over her. She nestled a bit closer to his warmth and gave up the battle to stay awake. His lips pressed a kiss softly against her forehead and ushered her into a deep sleep.

* * *

Nestled in her princess bed, Carina had slept very well for a while. Now blinking into the darkness, she knew it wasn't time to get up yet. Thank goodness there was a nightlight in her room. Peering over the side of the bed, Carina tried to convince herself that she didn't need to go to the bathroom. The bed was so high up and she was so groggy.

Her bladder informed her she couldn't wait. Carina rolled onto her tummy to try scooting off the bed toes first. As her weight landed on her abdomen, Carina gasped, "Oh!" The pressure on her full bladder made her almost wet herself. Rolling to her side she frantically pressed her thighs together, calling for help, "Daddy?"

"Come on, Little one." Luca seemed to appear instantly. Without asking a single question, he lifted her from the bed and carried her swiftly to the hall bathroom.

"How did you know I needed to go?"

"I heard your 'Oh,' and came to help."

"Thank you," she whispered.

After setting Carina on her feet, Luca swept the long nightgown up around her waist and held it securely as dropped to the toilet. He lounged against the vanity. His form easily viewed in the glow of the nightlight to his side. Luca's dark hair was ruffled. Her fingers itched to smooth it out.

To distract her thoughts, she blurted, "I'm sorry to wake you up, Daddy. I love my bed. It's so pretty but if I had a lower bed, I could get up by myself at night," she suggested.

"Your bed will stay at the height it is currently. Little girls don't need to be up at night without their Daddies. Call and I will come immediately. I am an extremely light sleeper."

Nodding automatically at his commanding tone, Carina couldn't help looking at his form. Dressed in his customary suit, Luca was devastatingly handsome. The finest fabric custom fit to his body hinted at his toned physique. Now, he wore only light cotton sleep pants. His bare chest in the revealed chiseled muscles that demanded to be explored. The shadows in the grooves of his flesh chased each other as he breathed evenly.

Tearing her gaze from that display, her focus lowered to his light-colored pajamas and froze. Luca's relaxed shaft pressed thickly against thin material. She must be seeing something incorrectly. He couldn't be that size, could he? As she watched, the generous bulge began to harden and lengthen.

"Your eyes are very big, Little girl." His deep voice startled her and she realized not only was she staring at his cock, he knew that she was focused on his attributes.

"Sorry!" Carina studied the tile under her feet.

She watched his bare feet approach. The rattling of the toilet paper roll made her look to the side. Luca gathered some in his hands and ripped it from the dispenser. Taking the paper, Carina quickly used it and popped up from the seat. She avoided his knowing eyes.

His powerful hand cupped her chin to raise her gaze to meet his. His expression revealed his desire. Luca didn't say anything. He just pulled her close to press their bodies together. Her breast flattened against his hard chest. Luca lowered his mouth to nip at her bottom lip. The brief shard of pain made her squeeze her thighs together as her body reacted to his closeness.

Unable to stop herself, Carina inhaled deeply. His scent was enticing. Masculine and enticing, Luca's natural aroma filled her senses. She chased his lips, rising to her toes to offer her lips to him. To her delight, he accepted her invitation. His lips pressed hers apart and his tongue explored her mouth, tempting her to join the intimate dance.

Ripping his mouth from hers, Luca growled, "Little girl, you are temptation incarnate." He set her away from him and took her hand. With a gentle tug to get her walking, Luca headed back to her nursery. Lifting her back into the elevated bed, he tucked her legs under the covers and pulled them up to her chin.

"Go back to sleep, Valentine. Don't hesitate to call if you need to get up. Doing so by yourself will result in a consequence," he warned.

The view of him walking away brought her up onto one elbow. Flopping back to the mattress when Luca disappeared into the darkness, Carina raised her eyes to the ceiling. She should have been intimidated by his size, but instead her fingers itched to wrap around his cock. When squeezing her thighs together to try to quell her arousal did work, Carina rolled around in bed to pull up the long nightgown. Her fingers had just dipped into her intimate juices when Luca's deep voice resounded through the nursery.

"No touching, Carina. Daddy is in control of your pleasure now. Hands above the covers," he ordered.

Staring at the teddy bear containing the baby monitor, Carina couldn't believe that Luca knew that she was pleasuring herself. Quickly, she moved her arms out of the covers and froze in place. How would she ever go back to sleep?

A thought popped into her mind, "Can he see me?" Immediately, she slammed her eyelids closed. To her amazement, sleep came quickly.

CHAPTER 9

"Good morning, Valentine." His deep voice wrapped around her, weaving into the erotic dream she enjoyed.

"Daddy. Touch me, please," she whispered as she moved restlessly on the crisp sheets.

"Wake up, Little one."

The dip of the bed under his weight registered that this couldn't be a dream. Looking up, Carina met Luca's amused gaze. "Morning," she said quickly, hoping she hadn't said aloud what she thought she had.

"Did you sleep well?" he asked, running a finger along her cheek.

"I slept like a dead person. Especially, in a new place, I don't usually sleep very well."

"Nurseries are magical places. I had a feeling that you and Daffy would sleep well here."

Reminded of her stuffie, Carina pushed up on her elbows to look around. Her kitten wasn't anywhere on the bed. "Where's Daffy?" she asked in concern.

"Let's see." Luca stood up and walked around the high

bed. "Here she is. Daffy was sleeping under the bed to protect you."

"She fell all that way? Is she hurt?" Carina accepted her stuffed friend and turned her in all directions to check for injuries. Then, hugging Daffy tight, she said, "This bed is too high. It's dangerous. Could you lower it for us?"

"I will definitely make it safer for both of you," he replied. Luca removed his phone from his suit jacket and typed a quick message.

"You're all dressed up," she commented as her gaze ran over his body. She loved the sight of Luca in his business attire. Now that she'd seen him dressed in only sleep pants, she realized how formally he usually dressed.

"Do you ever wear jeans?"

"Yes, Carina. I wear jeans. But not today! We have a busy day. Today, we'll meet with the priest before the wedding and select the items you wish to keep from your apartment."

"I can't pack all my stuff in one day!" she protested.

"I didn't say that. Today, you will select the items you wish to keep from your apartment."

"Oh!" Thinking for a moment, she asked, "Is someone else going to pack up my apartment?"

"The items we don't select to take today will be donated to a charity for its thrift store."

"What if I don't want to do that? Couldn't it all be put in storage?"

"For the next sixty years or so?" he asked, quirking up an amused eyebrow.

The implication of his words underlined the message she had heard over and over from him. There was no escape. She was his now, forever. Carina stared at him.

"If something would happen to me, my family will always provide for you. The documents you signed contained that clause."

"What's going to happen to you? Are you ill?" she asked

quickly, scooting to kneel on the bed as her hands roamed over him in concern.

Trapping her arms against her body, Luca lifted her onto his lap. His lips captured hers in a tender kiss. "It pleases me that you are worried. There is nothing wrong with me, Little one. I do, however, live in a treacherous world. It is wise to take precautions."

"What is your job exactly," she asked.

"My family has been in power for many years. My job is to maintain our control."

Carina swallowed hard. She didn't like the sound of that. She'd been very sure to ignore the rumors about the Ricci family. "Are you one of the bad guys?"

"Only if forced," he answered. "Now, it's time for Little girls to be out of bed. You get to wear your big girl clothes today for our appointment with the priest."

"And a bra?" she asked worriedly.

"And a bra," he confirmed with a chuckle. Setting her toes on the thick carpet, he stood to take her hand. "Your adult clothes are in the master bedroom."

As he led her down the hall, she realized that meant he would know anytime she accessed whatever he had placed there. Luca would always be in control. A foreboding shiver went down her spine.

* * *

Carina studied the bronze door plaque containing Father O'Sullivan's name as they waited in the church office. The Irish American priest had concerned the mainly Italian neighborhood at first. The fact he had attended the same schools as most of the children had reassured everyone. His subsequent good works in the area quieted any negative comments.

Luca placed a hand over her twisting fingers. "It's okay,

Carina. The meeting is simply a formality. We will be on our way soon."

When the door opened, she jumped slightly. Schooling her expression, she rose to her feet when the priest invited them inside. Luca's warm hand on her lower back steered her gently inside.

"My congratulations to the two of you," Father O'Sullivan shared cheerfully as he closed the door and waved them into the chairs before his desk. "Tell me how you met," he requested.

"We were in school together," Carina supplied quickly.

"Carina has always been brilliant. She skipped two grades in elementary school. We hadn't seen each other for years until fate threw us back together," Luca added smoothly.

"I see. Sounds like a fairytale romance. Are you certain that you are both ready for marriage? Your request for a ceremony appeared rushed." The priest made a few notes before sitting back in his chair.

"We have been apart too long. I am eager to make Carina mine," Luca confessed.

"Marriage should not be rushed into without a great amount of thought. Are you both sure, you are ready for this step?" Father O'Sullivan asked, looking deliberately at Carina.

She cleared her throat delicately to give herself a second to decide how to respond. "Thank you, Father, for counseling us today. I'm sure you see a wide variety of couples sitting across from you. Luca and I fit together. He's the piece that has been missing from my life. When we reconnected, every-thing snapped into place."

Carina could tell from the priest's expression that her answer allayed his concerns. Luca took her hand and squeezed it gently. When she peeked up at him, he smiled. Unable to resist the allure of his handsome face, she felt the corners of her lips curl upward in an answering grin. As much as he had forced her into this marriage, she was drawn to him. She always had been.

The scribbling of a pen on paper drew her attention back to the man behind the desk. When he glanced up from his notes, the priest wore a different expression. "I like that metaphor. I think I'll steal it with your permission for the service." He looked at Carina.

"Of course," she rushed to say.

"I prefer to lead a traditional service but one that is not too long. Our elderly tend to fall asleep if I talk too long," he confided. "Do you have any special requests?"

"No, Father. We have no special requests. For us, a traditional service is perfect. Shorter is better. I do not wish to tire Carina with a long service," Luca assured the priest smoothly.

"I see that you will take excellent care of your bride. If you don't have any questions for me, I'll let you go take care all the last minute details," Father O'Sullivan said as he stood and offered his hand to Luca.

"Thank you, Father. Please acccept this contribution to the church." Luca withdrew a check from his pocket and handed it to the priest. The recipient's wide eyes confirmed for Carina that the check was very generous. "A personal gift will come for you later this afternoon."

"That is unnecessary," the priest began, but his protests were waved off by Luca.

"It is our pleasure to have you celebrate our wedding, Father." Turning to Carina, he suggested, "Shall we?" She nodded and preceded him out the door.

With a wave to the church secretary, Carina allowed Luca to guide her back to the car. As he drove from the parking lot, she asked, "What did you send him for a personal gift?"

"A bottle of the finest Irish whisky."

"Do priests drink?" she asked, bewildered.

"Father O'Sullivan does."

"Are there no secrets you don't know?"

"All secrets can be uncovered with the correct motivation."

"Even yours?"

"No, mine are kept under lock and key," he answered with a laugh. "Enough of this serious conversation. Breakfast and on to your apartment."

CHAPTER 10

C arina sagged against Luca as he carried her into their wing. She hadn't been so exhausted in a very long time. He hadn't allowed her to work hard, but the emotional impact had been very difficult. As a poor teacher, she'd had to work hard for everything she owned. Everything was important to her.

She knew it was hard for Luca to understand how she felt. He didn't care about her copper bottom skillets. Luca didn't understand that she'd saved her extra pay for tutoring over six months to afford them. But that was just stuff.

Her pictures and family treasures went into boxes that his moving staff carried away—somewhere. When she opened her underwear drawer, it was empty. She remembered the supply of her things already in the large dresser in the master bedroom. The thought of a stranger going through her intimate things was unsettling. Luca did not understand.

"My staff is well trained to take care of a variety of tasks. My instructions were for one of the women to deal with your clothes."

The thought of something else made her rush to the bedside table. She waited for the mover to carry two of the overly bright pictures she'd found by the dumpster out of the room before she opened the drawer. It was empty. Horrified, she looked up at Luca.

"I picked up your vibrator and your tablet after you went to sleep last night. I also picked up your lingerie and a few outfits." He gestured to the simple dress, he'd chosen for her to wear to the church that morning.

"They didn't touch my stuff?" she double-checked.

"I took care of your privacy," he assured her.

The thought of him collecting her vibrator and the other things in that drawer embarrassed her, but better him than the staff efficiently clearing her apartment. "Thank you," she whispered.

"Of course, Valentine. Now, let's choose those things most important to you and we'll let the rest to the movers. There is no rush. Consider what you would miss the most."

Immediately, Carina went to the living room and picked up the crocheted afghan stretched over the back of the couch. "My grandmother made this for me," she explained and then turned in circles trying to figure out what to do with it.

"Allow me, Carina," Luca said, stepping forward to take it from her hands. A mover immediately provided him with an empty box.

Carina looked around the room to see what else she wanted. Picking up the scrapbook with the precious letters her students had written to her as well as her school pictures, she handed that to Luca. He placed it in the box without comment. She looked around at the small knickknacks that she'd collected over the years and dismissed those. A flash of light caught her eye. Walking to the sliding glass door onto the patio, she carefully removed the crystal and its suction hook hanger. Carina loved the beautiful rainbow reflections it scattered around.

"I think one of the big windows in your nursery would be

the perfect spot for that," he said with a smile and an outstretched hand. "I'll put it in my pocket so it isn't lost."

"Thank you." She searched his face for any sign that he was making fun of her and found only sincerity. Her mood lightened, she turned back to search the room for her next treasure.

Going through the apartment drained her emotionally. Trying to assign a value to everything she owned was daunting. When she'd found herself randomly picking up things and setting them down, Carina knew that she was done. She took one last tour through every room and returned to Luca's side. He was waiting patiently doing business on his phone. The moment she arrived, he tucked his cell into his pocket. She smiled at his action.

Luca always preferred her to his phone. In a world ruled by electronic devices, she found it incredible that he put her first. Heavens knows she'd spent a few dates looking at the back of someone's phone.

"Anything else to add?"

"I'll need my makeup for the wedding," she answered quickly.

"Here you are, Mr. Ricci. I just gathered it for you," a feminine voice assured him.

Carina looked at the woman, batting her eyelashes at Luca. He always had attracted women. She started to look away when he thanked the packer and accepted the box without another word. Her gaze darted to his face expecting that she'd catch him checking out the woman's tight jeans. To her astonishment, he was folding the box top closed to place it next to her special memories collection.

Looking up, he smiled at her when he found her watching him. "Make one more trip around the apartment. Double check that you have everything you want."

Immediately, she turned to follow his command. Again, he allowed her privacy to go through the apartment. Stepping into the empty closet, she hesitated, looking at the empty shelves. Something was lurking in the back of her mind. What was she missing? An ornate box popped into her mind. Quickly, she returned to the charismatic man waiting patiently for her.

"Luca? Did you take my jewelry box to the house?"

"Jewelry box? No, I haven't seen it. Where did you keep your jewelry?"

"It was in the closet on the shelf between the hanging clothes on the right," she described, closing her eyes to pull up a picture in her mind to pinpoint the location.

"Brian, could you check for me if Carina's jewelry box was delivered with her clothes while we finalized the ceremony?" Luca's sharp voice made her open her eyes to focus on him.

She could hear the muffled response through the cell phone in Luca's hand. The hardening expression on Luca's face was all she needed to see to know he was very displeased. She'd never seen that look. It scared her.

Sliding his phone back into his inner jacket pocket, Luca snapped, "Marco!"

A man arrived at his side in seconds. "Yes, Mr. Ricci."

"Who packed Ms. Richmond's closet?"

"Sherry gathered all the clothes and coats in the apartment. Is there a problem?"

"My fiancée's jewelry box was not delivered with her clothing."

The man shuffled through the sheets on his clipboard. "The staff is trained to bring anything to me that is valuable for special handling. I log it here. I do not have a jewelry box listed." Marco turned to the jumble of personal items by the door and walked to pick up a black backpack. Opening it, he removed a fanciful box decorated with fake jewels, silver, and gold beads. Without a word, he handed it to Luca.

"Carina, would you look through this and see if everything is here?" Luca asked, handing the box to her. Nodding, Carina took it and sat down on a nearby chair to open the lid and look through the contents.

"Call Sherry into the room, please."

The young woman who had flirted with Luca appeared in the doorway. Upon seeing her open backpack in Marco's hands, her expression froze. She turned to flee the apartment, but one of the large laborers carrying the heavy items from her apartment blocked the door.

Slowly, Sherry turned around to face them. She didn't try to say anything. Carina watched her swallow hard, before ducking her head down to examine the contents of the box on her lap. Based on Luca's coldly furious expression, Carina was frightened for the employee. A smaller part of her was simultaneously pissed that Sherry had tried to take her things.

Out of the corner of her eye, Carina watched Marco dump the remaining contents of each pocket in the bag onto the coffee table. Tampons, a wallet, and various personal items rained down. She saw Luca pick up the wallet and remove her driver's license to take a picture and fiddle on his phone. Carina knew immediately that he had sent that photo somewhere.

With that task done, he looked at Carina. "Do you see anything that is missing?"

"My grandmother's watch. It's not important, Luca. I'm sure it's not worth anything."

Marco demanded, "Empty your pockets, Sherry."

"I'm sorry. I thought you would throw out the costume jewelry. My daughters like to play princess. I should have asked," Sherry rushed to explain.

Neither man's expression changed. Marco repeated, "Empty your pockets."

Sherry slid trembling hands into pockets and pulled the fabric out. A silvery item tumbled to the floor. Marco retrieved it and handed it to his boss. "I'm sorry. I've worked for you, Mr. Ricci, for eight years. I've never taken anything." She turned to look at Carina who watched openly now.

"Miss Richmond, my daughter Kelly was in your class two years ago. Do you remember her? She has big brown eyes and loves to wear sparkly things."

"I do remember her. She had lovely manners and worked hard in class." Carina looked at her fiancé, and added, "Luca…"

"No, Carina. She stole from you and the Ricci family. This will not be tolerated." Turning back to Sherry, he added, "I could call the police and have you jailed for theft. In deference to my fiancée's tender heart, I will handle this another way."

"Thank you, Mr. Ricci." Sherry's voice wavered as she blinked her eyes rapidly.

To Marco, he directed, "Please escort Sherry from the building, Marco. She will not work for my family or our associates again."

Stiffening her spine, Sherry asked in a flash of courage, "Can I get my keys and my bus pass, please?"

"Of course. The Ricci family does not steal from others," Luca answered coldly. He placed her ID into the wallet and dropped it onto the table. He stepped back and sent a message from his phone.

When his gaze no longer pinned her in place, Sherry immediately scrambled forward to gather her possessions. After throwing everything into her backpack, she turned to apologize to Carina. "I'm sorry, Miss Richmond. You're an excellent teacher. I don't know why I was so stupid."

Carina didn't know what to say so she nodded. Watching Sherry shoulder her backpack and follow Marco toward the door. Just as she reached it, her cellphone rang. Sherry answered it as she walked down the hallway.

"You were fired?" Her voice drifted back in through the open door.

Her gaze flew to Luca. "What did you do?"

"Employees of the Ricci family do not steal. They will find it easier to move to a different city now."

"But they have two daughters," she protested.

"Your former students still have their mother. I did not call the police and have her taken to jail."

Swallowing hard, Carina nodded. She reminded herself that she could never expect Luca to be soft. The tenderness he had shown her did not apply to others. A thought flashed into her mind and she stepped closer to him. "Are you going to get rid of me if I'm bad?"

"No, Little girl. You belong to me now. If you do something wrong, you will earn consequences."

"Spankings?"

"Or worse.

CHAPTER 11

Arriving back at the Ricci estate, Carina felt drained. Her energy had been drained by the stress of meeting with the priest and deflecting his concerns about their last-minute wedding and the unpleasantness with Sherry. During the quiet car ride, she had almost drifted off to sleep several times, only jerking herself awake as she started to sag in her seat.

A large van announcing an exclusive bridal shop had parked at the main entrance. Luca stopped the car just behind them and came around to scoop Carina up in his arms. "Naptime, Little one."

"Mr. Luca, I've set up the bridal coordinators in the study. They are ready when Ms. Carina wishes to try on a selection of gowns," Brian greeted them and held the door for Luca to carry her inside.

"My Little needs to nap, Brian. We will have to try on gowns later," Luca instructed.

"Oh, they're here now. I can look at them now," Carina reassured him before stifling a yawn.

"I will speak to the coordinator," Brian answered and excused himself.

"We can't ask them to stay while I take a nap." Carina leaned away from Luca's hard body.

"Settle down, Little girl. You don't want to have a red bottom when you take your clothes off to try on gowns," Luca reminded her as he carried them toward his wing of the house.

Carina froze in his arms. "You wouldn't! Someone would report you for beating me."

"That will not happen. If you've obviously been spanked, everyone will realize that you've been bad. Do you want everyone to know?"

"No!" Carina crossed her arms in front of her chest and huffed in exasperation.

Luca did not respond. Carrying her directly to her nursery, he set her on her feet. "Big girl clothes off." He pulled her dress over her head and quickly eliminated her bra and panties. When Carina breathed a sigh of relief after being released from the bra, Luca kissed her shoulder gently. "Do you need to potty?"

"Please." Carina followed him down the hallway and used the toilet as he lounged by the vanity. It seemed bizarre that the horror she'd felt in having to use the restroom in front of Luca had faded to self-consciousness. Soon, she laid in his arms to rock and drink a bottle of formula.

He held her nude body in his arms so gently. Carina loved being close to his hard body and the power contained in his form. She wanted to be mad that he had taken the choice from her to try on gowns, but he was right. She was exhausted. This time she didn't even try to stay awake.

* * *

Blinking into the bright afternoon light filling the nursery, Carina jackknifed to seat on the comfortable bed. "Daddy? I'm awake." A knock on her door, and it opened to reveal Luc with a tray.

"Hi, Little one. Did you sleep well?

"I guess I was tired," she confessed.

"I brought you a snack to eat before finding the perfect gown. Let me help you down from bed." He lifted her easily from the bed and set her down. "Let's see... To try on clothes, you need panties." He opened a drawer and pulled out a pair of white cotton underwear. Kneeling in front of her, he dressed her. "And a robe." He opened the closet at the end of the room and removed a pink terrycloth robe.

After helping her thread her arms into the garment, he asked, "Are you hungry?"

Her growling stomach answered for her. With a chuckle, he pulled out a chair at the small two-person table and emptied the tray. A plate of sandwiches and a bowl of strawberries with whipped cream. Luca placed a half sandwich on her plate and three strawberries with a heaping spoon of whipped cream.

"Yum!" she hummed dipping the strawberry back into the whipped topping. "I think this is made from real cream. It definitely doesn't come from a plastic tub," she commented, focused on the strawberry.

"Eat your sandwich, too," he reminded her.

After popping the last bite of the strawberry into her mouth, Carina picked up the sandwich and took a big bite. She looked around the room and mumbled, "I need a clock in here."

"Nurseries and clocks do not go together," he answered, helping himself to sandwich half.

She swallowed hard in indignation and got choked. Coughing desperately, Carina panicked and looked at Luca for help. Immediately, he pulled her from the chair and hooked a finger into her mouth to yank the bread away. Air rushed back into her lungs as sagged against Luca's hard frame.

Holding her close, he sat back down on the chair and rocked her slowly. "Little girl, you've just entered my life full-time, I won't lose you now."

"That was so scary. I couldn't breathe. Thank you for helping me." She coughed quietly against his shoulder and felt his hand pat her firmly between the shoulder blades.

"Sit back and take a small sip. Let's make sure your throat is clear now," he commanded. Leaning away from her, he reached for a pink, sippy cup filled with juice and held it to her lips. Luca observed as she took several sips and swallowed.

"I'm okay, Daddy. I promise. No more sandwiches."

"No more sandwiches. Can I tempt you with a few more strawberries?" Luca reached for a strawberry and dipped it into the whipped cream. Holding it to her lips, he warned, "Small bites, Valentine."

After following his directions, she chewed slowly and swallowed. "Those are so good." Eagerly, she took another bite of the strawberry he held. When that one was finished, he offered another. This time, he popped the remainder of the strawberry into his mouth.

"Daddy! That one was mine," she protested.

"I like strawberries, too. You'll share, won't you?"

Of course, she nodded and opened her mouth for the next bite. Between the two of them, the bowl of strawberries emptied quickly. "We should have put more whipped cream on each strawberry," Carina commented as she scooped a fingertip through the remaining fluff in the bowl. Lifting her finger toward her lips, she hesitated and then, offered the sweet treat to Luca.

He didn't hesitate to sample the bite. His tongue swirled around her finger, reminding her of finesse in pleasing her so many ways. When her face heated, Luca released her index finger with a chuckle. "I'll have to remember your love of whipped cream."

"Daddy!"

"Come on, Little one. Time to go try on dresses. My mother would like to help you. She loves fashion. She also believes strongly in the old wives' tale that it is bad luck for the groom to see the bride before the wedding. For her, that includes the dress."

"Oh?" Carina thought furiously. She didn't want to offend her future mother-in-law before the wedding but what if she liked something awful.

"Mother has great style and flair. She has also been warned that this is your choice. I think you will find that she helps."

"Okay," she nodded. "When are they coming back?"

"They're waiting for you now. Are you ready?"

"Yes!" Carina was appalled that they were waiting for her. Surely, their time was more important than hers. She jumped off Luca's lap and tugged him toward the door.

"Carina, there is no rush. The coordinator and her staff are getting paid by the hour. Brian has taken great care of them as they waited. They are not unhappy," he assured her as he rose to walk leisurely toward the connecting door to the main room.

He paused for a few minutes to pick up the phone and press the purple button. A few seconds later, he spoke. "Dad, we're headed down for Carina to try on gowns. She'd welcome mom's assistance if she'd care to join us."

* * *

"That's the one," Elizabeth Ricci whispered as soon as the long row of buttons was fastened.

"It is exquisite, but it has to cost a fortune. All these crystals!" Carina twisted back and forth in front of the mirror as the gems shot prisms of light in all directions. "Is the back as pretty as I think?" she asked, looking over her shoulder at the mirror strategically placed behind her.

"Gorgeous!" her future mother-in-law rushed to assure her.

"It sounds like you've made your decision. The dress is absolutely stunning on you, Carina. Luca will lose his mind when he sees you walking down the aisle. It's a unique combination of innocence and sensuality," the wedding coordinator observed.

"I'm not sure if the price is right. How much is this dress?" Carina asked, biting her lip. Unable to tear her eyes away from her reflection, she stared at herself. *Is this really me?*

"All the dresses were approved by Luca, Carina. You don't have to worry how much each one costs," Elizabeth assured her.

Carina turned to study her future mother-in-law's face. Seconds later, she nodded. "This is the one. I love it."

"I will step outside and let Mr. Ricci know you have made a selection and I will send the alterations expert in to see if anything needs to be adjusted before the ceremony." The coordinator disappeared from the room.

The second the door snicked closed, Bethy rushed forward. "I'm so glad you like this dress. You're absolutely beautiful. Turn around and watch it swirl."

Carina allowed herself to grin back. "I feel like a fairy princess and the queen all wrapped together in one package." She twirled, laughing in enchantment as the light reflected on all the crystals. Without thinking, she held out her hands to the other Little girl. It didn't matter that she was her mother-in-law. As Bethy took her hands to jump up and down in joy with her, Carina knew that the other Little would be a friend.

CHAPTER 12

That evening, she sat cuddled against Luca's chest. He'd wrapped his arms around her to hold her close. Carina felt cared for and protected. Under her ear, she could feel Luca's heart beat in a slow, even beat. She felt closer to him than anyone ever.

"Luca?"

"Yes, Little girl?"

"Will you ever let me teach again?"

"For our children, of course."

"We'll have children? How will we do that… with me as your Little girl?"

"Just as our intimate play would be private from their knowledge, your role as my Little will be private as well. Our space is large enough here for a baby's nursery and teenagers' rooms later. I grew up knowing that my father was in charge and that their relationship was close and different from my friends."

"Didn't it bother you?"

"No. My parents love each other and they love me. Now, they are learning to love you as well. Nothing else matters." His arms tightened around her.

"I had fun with Bethy today. We both loved my gown."

"I'm glad. I look forward to seeing it. Did it have a low back?" Luca drew his fingers lightly down her spine to stop just before her bottom.

"I can't tell you that! You'll have to wait," she protested, leaning back to look at his face.

"You can't blame a groom for trying," he teased.

Staring at his amused face, Carina marveled at all the sides to Luca. From the stern Daddy who spanked her and treated her stomach to the light-hearted man who held her, Luca was not what she had expected. "Who are you really?" she whispered in confusion.

"I am your Daddy. I am here to love you when you are naughty and when you follow my directions."

"You love me?"

"I had one card to give out in my life. I've loved you since the eighth grade."

"But you dated all those other women!"

"You weren't ready for me. I've always been in your life, watching over you. You just didn't see me."

"My apartment? Did you get them to lower my rent?" She'd been so excited to find a place that she could afford on a beginning teacher's salary. Every other place she'd toured had been in risky neighborhoods. An invitation to come tour the newly built complex had landed in her inbox. Curious, she'd made an appointment, knowing that she couldn't afford it. When they'd offered her a place in her price range, she'd jumped on it.

"Your apartment is part of the Ricci properties."

Unable to decide whether she should be pissed or pleased, Carina pressed her cheek back to his chest. The steady thump of his heart reassured her that he was just a man. "A Daddy," she corrected herself.

"Tomorrow will be very busy. You have a variety of appointments before the wedding."

"I'd like to get my nails done," she suggested, sitting up straight once again. She covered her mouth as she yawned.

"That is on the list. For now, it's time for a quick shower and bedtime."

"All I do is sleep," she protested.

"Little girls need their rest. Come, tonight Daddy will join you in the shower."

"Really?"

Luca stood with Carina up on her feet before uncurling from the couch. He led her through the master bedroom into the immense bathroom. She felt her face heat when he stopped by the large ottoman where he had restrained her during her enemas. The built-in restraints lay unfastened against the leather. She turned around quickly, and Luca's hands closed over her shoulders to keep her in place.

"No stomach treatment today," he promised. Stepping away, he turned on the water in the shower before returning to her.

When he drew her T-shirt over her head, Carina cooperated. Although she was adjusting to his care, Carina felt her face heat as Luca's gaze traced over her body. When he knelt at her feet to whisk her leggings down her legs, she daringly stroked her fingers through his thick, black hair. He rewarded her with a kiss on one thigh.

"Step, Little girl," he directed. The comfy pants and her underwear soon rested with her top on the padded ottoman. Luca leaned closer to her body and pressed a kiss to the curls at the apex of her legs. He inhaled her intimate scent deeply before ruffling his fingers through her pubic hair. "This will go tomorrow as well."

"Really?" she squeaked. She knew friends who frequently went to salons for waxing. For Carina, it sounded scary and personal.

"You will have a busy day tomorrow. Go get in the shower, Little one. I will be there soon."

Obediently, Carina jumped in the shower and adjusted the water just a bit. Turning to the transparent wall into the bathroom, she froze in place. Luca's shirt had already joined hers. As she watched, he unzipped his pants and pushed his underwear and slacks to the ground. When the barrier began to fog, she wiped her hand over the panel to see clearly.

Luca faced the center of the room. Her gaze slid over his toned back to linger on his butt. Athletically rounded, Carina savored the view as he folded his pants. Forcing her eyes downward, she appreciated his muscular legs. He was handsomely formed.

When he turned to stalk forward, she scanned his body. Her gaze jumped over his muscled abs. His cock bounced slightly as he walked. As she watched, it began to lengthen and stiffen. Hypnotized, she couldn't tear her gaze away as he entered the shower stall. Carina's mouth rounded in a silent O as she watched Luca wrap his fingers around the thick shaft and stroke its length.

"Little girl, you have very big eyes," Luca commented.

Embarrassed, she looked at his face quickly. "Sorry!" she whispered before turning back toward the spray. Carina dipped her face into the water.

His arm wrapped around her body as he stepped closer. Pulling her backward to remove her features from the liquid, Luca pressed his body against hers. His thick cock thrust against the seam of her buttocks. Carina looked over her shoulder. Luca's expression was fierce. He lifted his free hand to cup her chin and hold it steady as her Luca captured her lips in a searing kiss.

When he lifted his lips from hers, they both gasped for breath. Carina stared at him in wonder. No one had ever looked at her like Luca did. It was as if she were prey that he hunted for his survival. She shivered against his warmth. "Little girl," he exhaled. "You are temptation incarnate. Soon, I will pin you against the tiled wall as I go so far deep inside you, you won't know where you end and I start."

"Luca…" she whispered, caught in his web of passion and attraction.

He moved against her bottom. Thrusting between her buttocks, Luca made sure she felt every inch of his large penis. A moan fell from her lips as her body responded to him. Carina reached behind her body to run her hands over his sides and anything else she could reach. She protested with "No," as he moved away.

"Shower and bed tonight," he reminded her. Filling his hand with liquid soap scented of lavender, Luca began to smooth it over her body. Caressing every inch of her flesh, he washed her as she explored his chest and arms with her lips and hands.

When her fingers glided over his abs, Luca trapped her hand against him, "No touching Daddy's penis without permission, Valentine."

"Really?" she repeated exasperated when Luca set rules in place for what seemed like the hundredth time.

His chuckle made her angry and she lashed out slapping his chest with one open hand. The sound echoed through the large chamber. Instantly sorry, she backed away and apologized, "Sorry. I shouldn't have done that."

"Put your hands against the tile, Carina."

"Don't spank me, please!" she pleaded.

"Hands on the wall now."

Walking through the shower spray to get there, she blindly waved her hands before her. When her fingertips struck the tile, she leaned against it. She rubbed her face against her biceps to wipe the water from her eyes. Looking back over her shoulder, she watched him walk out of the shower and return seconds later with a silver object in his hand.

"No, Luca!"

"Daddy," he corrected as he lubricated the anal plug with liquid soap.

"Don't put that in me. I said I was sorry."

"This was going in your tight bottom tonight to start training you to accept me. Stand still. If I have to restrain you, I'll insert additional cleanser." He switched off the water to avoid rinsing it clean before he approached.

Carina froze in place as he spread her buttocks and pressed the blunt tip of the plug against her tight rosette. Immediately, the soap began to sting and she bucked toward the tile. When he didn't say anything, she peeked over her shoulder to see that he was adding more soap. Quickly she understood that each time she resisted, her punishment would increase. Carina pushed her bottom out, presenting herself.

Again, he separated her cheeks. His silence increased her discomfort. Seconds ticked by and finally, her Daddy pressed the rounded end against her tight ring of muscles. This time, she bit her lip as he pushed it into her body. She steeled her muscles not to squirm as the stinging intensified.

"Take a deep breath, Valentine." Luca waited for her to follow his directions. "Now, exhale in a big gust." As she blew out, he slid the thickest section into her bottom without hesitating.

"Ahh! It stings, Luca! Take it out!"

"There are consequences for your actions. Stand still and I'll finish your shower." When he turned on the water, she automatically stood up.

"Back into position."

Watching him over her shoulder, Carina reached for the wall once again. As soon as she leaned forward, he stroked the fragrant soap over her back. His touch was firm-caressing, yet efficient. She could feel his hard cock pressing against her when he leaned over her body. Finished with her torso, Luca squatted at her feet to suds her legs.

"Please," she whispered, meeting his gaze.

Without answering her, Luca stroked up her legs to finish at her upper thighs. He rose to bracket her against the tile, wrapping one hand across her stomach to delve into her pink folds. She knew that he found her wet with slick juices as her body responded to his closeness and her punishment. Embarrassed, she dropped her forehead to the tile to hide as he washed her intimately.

A moan of protest escaped her mouth when those tantalizing fingers left her body. Rinsing her body with the detachable sprayer, he directed, "Turn around and close your eyes, Little one." When she complied, he washed her face quickly.

Luca lifted his hands from her body. Immediately, Carina missed his touch. She stood warmed by the shower spray as she heard him moving around. Peeking through slitted eyelids, she watched Luca washing his body. The sight of his hands smoothing over his hard flesh fascinated Carina. She wanted to touch him so bad.

Wrapping one large hand around his rigid shaft, Luca pulled strongly along its length. She must have made some noise because Luca immediately barked, "Close your eyes." With a snap, she squeezed her eyelids together.

The sound of him moving sent her imagination into overdrive. Her brain created a scene in her mind. His hand tugging on his thick cock. She could hear the sound of his breath coming quicker and his masculine groans. Air flowed over her body in waves signaling her that he moved. Each gust built erotic details in her brain. The shower pelted into her skin, keeping her nerve endings on edge. Squeezing the intruder inside her, Carina debated whether to follow his directions or give into the temptation to watch.

"Carina!" Luca shouted. His deep voice echoing into the enclosure.

Slapping her hands over her eyes to make sure she didn't

look, Carina begged, "Daddy! Daddy, please!" She didn't know what she was asking for—she only knew that Luca was the only source for what she wanted.

Something stepped between her and the shower spray. It was her only clue that he approached before he ran his hands over her shoulder. As Luca wrapped his arms around her, Carina bolted forward to slam into his body. He held her close and rocked her softly.

"You're a good Little, Carina. All is forgiven now."

"Can you take it out?"

"Yes, Valentine. Turn around and put your hands on the tile."

This time she flew to the wall and presented her bottom eagerly. He stroked a hand over her soft swells before parting her buttocks. With a slow twist, he removed the anal plug and set it aside. One hand pressed between her shoulder blades to hold her in place when she would have turned around. Luca stepped out of the spray of the shower to allow the water to cascade down her displayed crease. She moaned in delight as some of the stinging diminished.

"It still burns," she whispered.

"Daddy will help you, Little girl." He pressed two finger-tips at that tight entrance and splayed it open a bit. Directing the handheld shower head as she squirmed, he rinsed the soap from her entrance. "Your evening medicine should solve the rest."

"Thank you, Daddy." When Luca turned off the water, she asked, "Can I turn around?"

"Yes, Valentine. You are learning such good manners."

The sight of his smiling face made her heart swell. She didn't know why his opinion mattered so much. It just did. Distracted by her thoughts, Carina allowed Luca to guide her from the shower stall. He dried her body with a soft towel before wrapping a fresh, warmed one around her.

Suddenly, she lunged to the toilet. Several embarrassing

moments later, Luca helped her from the seat. Her knees were weak from the force of her bowels emptying. "I must be sick," she whispered as he lifted her into his arms.

"The soap has a secondary effect, Valentine. You will be better in the morning."

"Promise?"

"I promise."

She didn't fight as he dosed her bottom with the two suppositories and smoothed cooling cream inside her. Luca took control of everything without hesitation. When he dressed her in the soft nightgown and tucked her in the high princess bed with Daffy into her arms, she didn't protest. Carina turned and snuggled into the soft mattress on her tummy.

A clicking noise made her open her eyes slightly. As she blinked sleepily, she saw a barrier rise into place on the side of the bed. Reaching out, she touched cold metal bars. Carina pulled her hand back into the warmth of the bedding. She'd worry about everything tomorrow.

CHAPTER 13

C arina stood before the large mirror in the master bedroom. Yesterday had been a whirlwind of appointments and activities. Every inch of her body had been plucked, polished, or massaged. Some had been painful—others perfectly relaxing.

Luca had tucked her into the large bed and stayed until she fell asleep. When she woke that morning, she was alone. A phone call to Brian had resulted in breakfast and the arrival of the stylists.

Now, Carina stared at herself in the mirror. She looked beautiful. As she started to pinch herself to make sure this was real, cool fingers closed her hand.

"No bruises. Your Daddy will spank you," Bethy leaned close to warn Carina with a shake of her head.

"This is really happening?" Carina whispered privately.

"It is. You make a gorgeous bride, Carina. But, you are as pretty inside as outside. I am very happy to have you in the family. Luca chose his Little girl very well."

"Thank you, Bethy." Carina squeezed her hand.

Mr. Ricci arrived at the door. "Bellissima! Luca will lose his mind seeing you walk down the aisle. Now, it is time to get into the limo to go to the church. What can I carry?" With the skill, Luca's father quickly steered everyone into the sleek limousine, waiting at the front door.

The scenery blurred in front of her. Carina began to panic. She squeezed Bethy's hand.

"Quickly, turn the air conditioner cooler and increase the fans back here," Mrs. Ricci ordered the driver as she squeezed Carina's hand. Leaning close, she whispered, "You have feelings for my son?"

"Yes."

"You trust that he will take care of you?"

"Y…yes," Carina hesitated on that one remembering the spankings that she had endured.

"He fills a hole within you that only a Daddy can?"

Startled, Carina sat up a bit taller. She raised her eyes from her hand tracing the beautiful crystals on her gown. "Yes."

"You feel special in your nursery?"

"Yes," Carina answered, feeling the corners of her mouth curl upward.

"Then, you are doing the right thing," Elizabeth Ricci suggested quietly. Then continuing at a regular volume, she added, "And besides, I can't wait to see those damn crystals sparkle in the light of the cathedral."

"Bethy," a deep voice warned upon hearing the curse word..

The two Littles burst into giggles and Carina sat back against the comfortable seat for the first time. The cool air swirled around her, lowering her body temperature back to a comfortable level. She turned to meet Bethy's gaze and mouthed, "Thank you."

Her future mother-in-law winked conspiratorially at her.

* * *

The music swelled in the large church and the wedding coordinator clued Carina to begin walking slowly. With her hands full of the exquisite bouquet of the special, pink roses and gardenias, she exhaled fully and took a deep breath. The first step was the hardest. Several others followed before Carina turned the corner and stepped onto the red carpet runner.

Her eyes fixed on Luca. He looked magnificent in the well-tailored tuxedo. He smiled at her and she couldn't resist returning it. She'd missed him this morning. Carina didn't know how she'd become so accustomed to having him with her so quickly. She just knew she felt better with Luca.

A flicker of light caught her eye, Carina looked around to see sparkles of light reflecting on the carpet at her feet. She felt like a fairy princess as she walked through the crowded church. Carina looked up and hoped her mother in heaven could see her walking down the aisle. Blinking hard, she looked back at Luca. The sight of the handsome man wiped sad thoughts from her mind. Passing Elizabeth Ricci, she stifled a laugh at the woman's joyful expression. Bethy needed a sparkly dress as well.

At the altar, Luca took her hand and kissed it. "You look beautiful, Valentine."

The ceremony was quick as they had requested. A blur of words to repeat and vows to take. Luca slid a beautiful ring onto her finger and leaned in to kiss her gently at first and then once again with a hint of restrained passion. To her delight, his eyes promised her everything.

Luca steered her down the aisle and into a private room. There, he pulled her into his arms and claimed her with kisses. A knock on the door sounded and Luca visibly forced himself away from her. "Little girl, you are an enchantment I can't resist in that dress. That was my favorite, but they didn't allow me to see which one you had chosen."

"It is enchanting," she agreed with him.

"We have to take pictures before the reception. Let me fix your lipstick." He withdrew a handkerchief from his pocket and wiped the smudge color from her face.

"Let me return the favor," she teased, tugging it from his hand before he could stuff it in his pocket. Carina wiped the transferred makeup from his face with a laugh.

"Thank you, Valentine." Luca dipped his head to kiss her again when the second knock interrupted him. "Come on, Little girl. Soon, there will be no interruptions."

Taking her hand, Luca walked confidently out the door, ignoring the people gathered around. He obviously didn't care if everyone knew what they had been doing. Carina tried to keep from blushing as the makeup artist clucked in dismay as she restored her lipstick and smoothed on additional powder.

Finally, their pictures as bride and groom and with family were complete. Luca had taken advantage of their closeness to touch her subtly. Her body felt electrified by his closeness. She knew Luca would soon make her his completely.

The reception was a blur. She remembered Luca insisting she try the delicious food. When it came to the cake cutting, Carina wished with all her heart that he wouldn't smash cake on her face as some brides and grooms treated each other. To her delight, he delicately placed a bite at her lips and allowed her to taste the delicious concoction. She returned the favor and laughed in delight as he deliberately nipped her fingertips.

Held securely in his arms, Carina loved dancing with Luca. As with everything he did, her new husband moved with skill and style. He showcased her in his arms, bringing barely whispered comments from the other dancers and the audience. Their spoken thoughts that she and Luca were a perfect couple and how much the groom obviously loved the bride reassured Carina.

"It is time for us to leave, Valentine."

"Now? Everyone is still here," she protested, looking at the crowd. People packed the dance floor, bar, and buffet.

"They will continue to enjoy our hospitality. The staff will take care of them." Taking her hand, Luca led her through a backdoor to his running car. Brian stood near with the keys.

"My congratulations, Mr. and Mrs. Ricci."

"Thank you, Brian," Carina remarked as Luca tucked her and the beautiful gown into the passenger seat.

In moments, they were on the road. Carina stroked her hand over the crystals of her wedding dress. "I loved this dress, Luca. It was such a lovely wedding. Thank you."

"Daddy," he reminded her. "You took my breath away, Valentine as you appeared in the aisle." He took her hand and squeezed it gently.

"You looked very elegant, yourself, Daddy. I hate that I can't wear this dress anymore. It was so expensive for one day."

"Cost is not important, Little girl. Perhaps, we should put it in your closet for you to play dress up? There is a ballroom on the estate for dancing."

Eagerly, she turned in her seat to look at him. "I'd love that, Daddy."

"I would, too, Carina." Luca squeezed her hand once again.

A comfortable silence filled the car as he maneuvered it through the darkened street. Pulling up in front of their home, Luca turned the key fob over to an attendant before lifting her from her seat. He carried her through the common areas to their private wing and straight to the master bedroom.

"I can wait no longer to make you mine, Carina. Turn around and hold very still. I do not wish to rip your dress."

Carina nodded and twirled around. Struggling to organize her conflicting thoughts, she squeezed her thighs together as her body responded to his touch as the back of her dress separated as he worked. Since she'd returned the card, one part of her wanted to rail against his control. The other reveled as he brought her fantasies of being a Little girl to life.

She smiled into the quiet room when he kissed the curve of her neck. Luca cared for her. He understood her. Would she rebel at times? Carina had no doubt that she would earn her Daddy's consequences regularly.

"Luca?"

"Daddy," he corrected.

"Daddy, are we going to be happy?"

"As soon as I get these damn buttons unfastened, I'll show you just how good we will be," he swore through gritted teeth. "You couldn't have loved a dress with a zipper?"

Laughing, Carina turned back to look at Luca. "You could tear it," she suggested.

"No, Valentine. Just like any incredible present, you are worth unwrapping delicately."

His gaze rose to meet hers and she shivered at the depth of desire reflected in his striking blue eyes. Her breath caught in her throat. She nodded without knowing what she agreed with and he rewarded her with a hot kiss against her spine.

Finally, the last button slid free. Luca helped her shimmy out of the dress before lifting her from the crumpled garment. He placed her delicately on the soft comforter before proceeding to shed his elegant tux and shirt. Stalking forward, he crawled onto the bed caging her under his fit body.

"These have to go," he growled, sitting back to hook his fingers under the sides of the only clothing she wore. Pulling sideways, Luca ripped away the scrap of lace wrapped around her hips. As his gaze roamed possessively over her displayed body, he held the damp panties to his nose and inhaled deeply.

"Luca," she whispered, caught in the sensuous web he weaved.

"Daddy, Little girl," he reminded her and caressed her bare mound with his fingertips, making her writhe below him as the super sensitized skin tingled at his touch.

His fingers traced the line of her sex. "Ah, Little one. You are eager for our joining," he remarked, lifting dripping fingers to his mouth. "Mmm," he hummed appreciatively as he moved back over her.

Capturing her lips, Luca shared her sweet flavor with Carina.

She responded to him eagerly. Tasting herself on his lips seemed to unlock the last of her reservations. Carina wrapped one hand around the back of his head to hold his lips against hers. Daringly, she swirled her tongue around his.

"Temptress," he growled before rewarding her with another fiery kiss that curled her toes.

Luca shifted to nibble down the sensitive length of her neck. His teeth fastened over the tender spot where it met her shoulder. Hearing the sharp inhale of her breath, he tightened his jaw slightly.

Carina wrapped her fingers around his wide shoulders and clung to his strength. The animalistic bite silently reminding her of his dominance. When he released her to smooth his tongue over the marked skin, she stroked her fingers through his thick, black hair.

Continuing his path down her body, Luca kissed a path along her breastbone. "You are so lovely, Valentine," he complimented against one soft mound. She jumped as his tongue wrapped around one nipple before he pulled it into the heat of his mouth. His hand caressed and gently kneaded her flesh. Desiring more, Carina arched her back to press her breast against him. He rewarded her with a brief nibble on the taut peak. With a pop of suction, Luca released the one he'd captured to taste her other nipple.

"Daddy! I want to touch you, too," she pleaded, trying to move her arms under his to caress his torso and lower. When he didn't answer, she added, "Please?"

To her delight, Luca wrapped his arms under her body and rolled on the bed to set her on top. She bent her knees to straddle him and pushed on his chest to sit astride him. Unable to resist, her body moved against his thick shaft, sliding it more intimately against her pink folds. They both groaned at the sensation. Her hands roamed over his chest and abdomen as his explored her body.

He is mine! As much as I am his, Luca now belongs to me!

"I don't know what you're thinking, Little one, but I like it." His voice was low and gravelly. "Kiss me, Valentine."

Neither could delay for long following that fiery kiss. Luca pulled a strip of condoms from under his pillow. When her eyes widened at the thought of them making love so many times, he chuckled. "I don't plan on letting you out of this room for a long time."

He allowed her to help him roll the protection over his thick erection. Inexperienced, she fumbled trying to stretch the sheathe over his large cock. When Luca took over, Carina bit her lip. His finger smoothed over her lip to rescue it.

"I'll fit, Valentine."

"Are you sure?" she double-checked.

"Yes." Luca leaned forward to kiss her lips. Distracting her with sweet kisses, he rotated their bodies once again, placing him on top.

She widened her thighs for him as he caressed her intimately. Circling her clitoris and her sensitive entrance, Luca seemed to know exactly where she needed his touch. When her hips bucked up against him asking for more, Luca slid two fingers into her tight entrance. Widening his fingers, he gently stretched her as he distracted her with tempting caresses and kisses adding additional lubricant to ease the way.

When she writhed underneath him, Luca removed his fingers and placed the head of his cock at her entrance. Slowly, he pressed inward. He stopped when her body tightened around him. "Little one, it's okay. Breathe."

Carina nodded and followed his directions. As her body eased around him, she felt Luca glide further inside. Deeper and deeper, he entered. Carina wrapped her legs around his waist, opening herself to him fully. Drawing a moan of pleasure from their throats, he thrust in fully.

He filled her entirely. Carina tightened her hands on his shoulders, overwhelmed by the sensation of him being part of her. When he moved, she could feel every inch of his shaft gliding against the sides of her tight channel. Unable to focus on anything other than the sensations of him moving in and over her, Luca became the center of her universe.

Their bodies strained together as their skin became slick with perspiration. Luca demanded everything from her and in response built the passion inside her body. His hand slid between their bodies to stroke over her clit.

"Come, Valentine," he commanded.

Her body obeyed. Pleasure skyrocketed through her as she clung to him. His body continued to move pushing those sensations even higher until she pleaded, "No more. I can't take it!"

"This is just the beginning, my Carina."

Abandoning herself to his control, she allowed herself to just feel. Again and again, he coaxed her into orgasms. Finally, Luca relinquished his iron-like control and he joined Carina as her body spasmed in bliss. His arms tightening around her, Luca's body shuddered over her as he poured himself into the condom. He held her close to him as they recovered. She loved the feel of his heart beating against her.

Carina felt empty when he glided from her. She wiggled a bit closer needing as much contact with this dynamic man as possible. Exhausted from his lovemaking and the stress of the wedding preparations, Carina allowed herself to sleep. In his arms, she would always be safe and protected.

EPILOGUE

Carina sat at the elegant dining table. The rich wood surface held sparking crystal and glimmering china. The chandeliers illuminated the room, chasing away the shadows. She wore her exquisite wedding gown as she grinned across the table at Bethy's eccentric formal attire. The plumed hat completed the look perfectly.

"Would you like some more tea, Daddy?" she offered, reaching for the heavy silver teapot.

"Stop right there, Valentine. Allow Brian to take care of that for you. I don't want you to be burnt," Luca corrected quickly.

"Okay, Daddy." Over the last two months, she had adjusted to addressing him with this name. She marveled at the changes that had happened in her life since returning that the card.

"Daddy, do you still have my card?" she blurted as the question leapt into her mind.

Luca reached into the breast pocket of his elegant suit to withdraw his telephone. Flipping open the front cover, he displayed the card in the space designed for a driver's license. It would be the first thing he saw. "I like to keep it close to my heart," he admitted as he slid it back into the interior pocket.

"You really aren't as mean as you pretend to be," she teased.

When she looked down to select another cookie from the tray Brian offered, Carina missed the pointed look that Luca shared with his father. There were some things that Little girls just didn't need to know.

Insulated from the world, Carina had adapted to her new life. Some things hadn't been easy to get used to, she thought as she squeezed her bottom muscles. With the challenges had come lots of wonderful treats as well. Being Luca's Little girl made her happy. She missed her job and the responsibilities of her grownup life less as time passed.

Luca spent as much time with her as possible. Alternating working in his home office and the large steel building in town, she worried about him working such long hours. When he'd allow it, Carina went to the office with him. She'd become addicted to the café mochas from the coffee shop downstairs when he needed privacy for a meeting or phone call.

Spending her time reading or learning to crochet an afghan like her grandmother's, Carina cherished the extra hours they spent together. While she didn't like the paddle in his desk, she adored the other toys he had stashed in the special Valentine box in that bottom drawer. Her Daddy always knew what she needed.

"Father?" Luca addressed the older man in formal attire. "Have you seen Dr. Hendrick's new insertable for Littles who behave badly?"

"I have not. Is it effective?"

"Extremely. You'll have to discuss it with him at your next appointment with him. He believes that sluggish tummies often lead to poor conduct. The doctor is recommending treatment with this filled plug after a spanking. Carina responded very well to it," Luca announced before waving Brian away as he offered his Little girl another cookie.

"Daddy!" Carina protested. She really wanted to try the white chocolate ones.

"No, means no," Luca answered raising one eyebrow in a silent message she'd learned to heed... most of the time.

She hadn't stopped pushing for information last night. She'd seen the young child's handwriting on the small envelope delivered to their wing. Her demands to read it had led to the experimentation with the doctor's new device. Only when she was squirming on a hot bottom with it implanted deep in her tight channel had she calmed down enough to explain why she wanted to read the card.

"Please, Daddy. I'm happy. I want to know that she is well. Then, I can put my former life behind me." Reading the short note aloud, Carina had learned that the surgery had been a success. Susanna was now recovering and would continue her treatment through next week. The threat of losing her sight was now very low. Carina had celebrated by snuggling close to her Daddy.

Drawn back to the present by a squeeze on her thigh, she scrambled to remember what he had said before answering quickly, "Yes, Daddy." Picking up her teacup with her pinky extended, Carina enjoyed the fragrant beverage. Challenging her father was not a wise chose. At the feel of his hand resting on her thigh, Carina smiled up at him. She really was lucky to be chosen by her Daddy.

Dr. Richards' Littles®

A beloved age play series that features Littles who find their forever Daddies and Mommies. Dr. Richards guides and supports their efforts to keep their Littles happy and healthy.

Available on Amazon

SANCTUM

Pepper North introduces you to an age play community that is isolated from the surrounding world. Here Littles can be Little, and Daddies can care for their Littles and keep them protected from the outside world.

Available on Amazon

Soldier Daddies

What private mission are these elite soldiers undertaking? They're all searching for their perfect Little girl.

Available on Amazon

The Keepers

This series from Pepper North is a twist on contemporary age play romances. Here are the stories of humans cared for by specially selected Keepers of an alien race. These are science fiction novels that age play readers will love!

Available on Amazon

The Magic of Twelve

The Magic of Twelve features the stories of twelve women transported on their 22nd birthday to a new life as the droblin (cherished Little one) of a Sorcerer of Bairn. These magic wielders have waited a long time to take complete care of their droblin's needs. They will protect their precious one to their last drop of magic from a growing menace. Each novel is a complete story.

Available on Amazon

ABOUT THE AUTHOR

Ever just gone for it? That's what *USA Today* Bestselling Author Pepper North did in 2017 when she posted a book for sale on Amazon without telling anyone. Thanks to her amazing fans, the support of the writing community, Mr. North, and a killer schedule, she has now written more than 70 books!

Enjoy contemporary, paranormal, dark, and erotic romances that are both sweet and steamy? Pepper will convert you into one of her loyal readers. What's coming in the future? A Daddypalooza!

Connect with me on your favorite platform! I'm also having fun on TikTok as well!

amazon.com/author/pepper_north
bookbub.com/profile/pepper-north
facebook.com/AuthorPepperNorth
instagram.com/4peppernorth
pinterest.com/4peppernorth
twitter.com/@4peppernorth

AFTERWORD

If you've enjoyed this story, it will make my day if you could leave an honest review on Amazon. Reviews help other people find my books and help me continue creating more Little adventures. My thanks in advance. I always love to hear from my readers what they enjoy and dislike when reading an alternate love story featuring age-play. Contact me on
my Pepper North FaceBook page,
on my website at www.4peppernorth.club
email at 4peppernorth@gmail.com

Want to read more stories featuring Zoey and all the Littles? Subscribe to my newsletter!
Every other issue will include a short story as well as other fun features! She promises not to overwhelm your mailbox and you can unsubscribe at any time.
As a special bonus, Pepper will send you a free collection of three short stories to get you started on all the Littles' fun activities!

Here's the link:
http://BookHip.com/FJBPQV

Follow me on BookBub for notifications of my new releases!

Printed in Great Britain
by Amazon

14195324R00079